GEORGINA AND GEORGETTE

By the same author

Address Unknown

GEORGINA AND GEORGETTE

by

MALCOLM HUTTON

ST. MARTIN'S PRESS
NEW YORK

For Susan, Kim and Lucy

Library of Congress Cataloging in Publication Data

Hutton, Malcolm.
  Georgina and Georgette.

  I. Title.
PR6058.U8598G4   1984   823'.914   84-13336
ISBN 0-312-32469-3

First published in Great Britain by Robert Hale Ltd.

First U.S. Edition

10 9 8 7 6 5 4 3 2 1

ONE

Two events were to mark that day in Tanniford. They were not connected with one another and each in its way was unique.

In Ferry Street, which had no pavements and where the front doors of the tiny terraced houses opened directly on to the narrow street, Billy Staton stood on the roof of his mother's car jumping up and down and shouting abuse at her. His mother sat, smoking and uncaring, on the front step of their house on the other side of the street, her legs stretched out into the road. She was three months pregnant with her second child.

As Billy bounced up and down, miraculously keeping his balance, the thin, pressed-steel roof made loud booming sounds which echoed up and down the short length of Ferry Street. The noises were highly satisfying to young Billy but to Mr Rose Cottage—who, for some reason, was known by the name of his house—the din was sheer torture. A few doors along he sat at his ground-floor front window as always, looking out and gibbering incomprehensibly as he daily drifted further into senility. He gesticulated wildly at Billy but Billy was used to the old man waving and mouthing and he took no notice.

Nearby, round the corner in Spring Street, the dustmen were gathered at the side entrance to the Spreadeagle. They had finished their rounds and were waiting to be admitted for their weekly tipple. The landlord unbolted the side door and they slipped inside. It was nine-thirty in the morning. Their large, yellow refuse vehicle was parked opposite, in the entrance to the shipyard. It would remain there for an hour or more while they slaked their thirst on this hot August morning. It was Tuesday . . . a normal Tuesday in Tanniford. Everyone knew the dustmen drank outside the permitted hours in the Spreadeagle. They did so every Tuesday. Even Ted Jordan, the local policeman who lived up the hill above the railway bridge, knew that. He did nothing about it though. One of the reasons Ted was popular in Tanniford was that he had the good sense not to interfere with customs that the villagers themselves accepted. For their part they very quickly let him know when they wanted anything doing about them.

On the other side of the village, in one of the cheap, weather-boarded houses in North Street, Gladys Haben-howe was entering the final stages of labour. The midwife had sent round to Ferry Street for Dr Oakleigh—something she rarely did because she took a pride in delivering the babies of Tanniford herself without the help of a doctor. In this case, however, there were signs of compli-cations to come and she was worried that there had been no ante-natal examination because Mrs Habenhowe had never attended a hospital, or a clinic, or seen a doctor.

"My mother didn't hold with doctors and hospitals," she told the midwife, "and she had four children—including me. She had them in this very room with no one to help her but the midwife and that's all the help I need."

Until a short time ago the midwife had been content to agree with her. But then, after listening with the foetal stethoscope, she'd made an internal examination and hurriedly sent for Dr Oakleigh.

Behind the closed doors of the Spreadeagle the dustmen had made today a special occasion. It was Sid's birthday. Sid was the driver.

"Foreman at depot gets cross if we're late back," Sid warned them.

"Ah, he do get out of his pram a bit sometimes," Stan allowed. "But it's yer birthday. C'mon . . . one for the road."

They had swallowed many more than 'one for the road' when they eventually rolled out of the Spreadeagle and staggered towards their vehicle. Sid mounted the lower of two steep steps to the driver's cab, his wavering hand, extended hopefully upwards, seeking the doorhandle. He missed the handle by several inches and fell on his back in the road, chortling helplessly. His team-mates stood around him also laughing. Sid lurched to his feet, pointed himself once more in the direction of the driver's door and made a crabwise run at it. This time he missed the door completely and ended up clinging to the front bumper.

"Tell you what," he hiccupped, dragging himself

upright. "You've got a licence, Stan. *You* drive the bloody thing."

Stan, no less drunk than Sid, but nursing a long-standing wish to drive the council's refuse vehicle, nodded his head solemnly. "I reckon I'd better," he said, swaying, " 'cos you're pissed, Sidney."

He made a better job of finding the doorhandle than Sid had done and clambered awkwardly into the driver's cab. Sid was guided by the other two men in the team to the door on the other side and pushed up into the cab alongside Stan. One of the men squeezed in beside him and the other one elected to 'ride on top', as he called it. What this actually meant was that he stood on the footplate at the tail-end of the vehicle where a notice proclaimed: RIDING ON THE REAR OF THIS VEHICLE IS STRICTLY FORBIDDEN. With much revving of the engine and crashing of gears the large, yellow dustcart lumbered off along Spring Street.

Dr Oakleigh reached the house in North Street just as Gladys Habenhowe, with a loud, gasping shriek, gave birth. When he entered the bedroom the midwife was staring in consternation at two tangled umbilical cords. The doctor stepped forward, took one look and said briskly: "You did absolutely right to call me."

As the refuse vehicle reached the corner of Ferry Street Sid, through a drunken haze, grasped that Stan was preparing to swing round into Ferry Street. He belched loudly and said:

"You can't take it down there, Stanley. You know we never go down Ferry Street."

It was true. From the time the first cars had started to be parked in the street after the war—even though they parked close against the fronts of the houses—the dustcart had stopped negotiating Ferry Street during its weekly collection. Instead, the householders were provided with large, black plastic bags into which they put their refuse and which the dustmen collected by hand each week. The milkman in his milk-float managed to squeeze past the parked cars but there was a deal of difference between the milk-float and the council refuse vehicle.

"Even I couldn't get through there," Sid told Stan. It was

a foolish thing to say because Stan had always considered himself a better driver than Sid and was now prompted to demonstrate his skill.

"Well, *I can*," he said confidently. " 'Sides, it's quicker than going along the High Street."

Sid closed his eyes as the dustcart surged forward into Ferry Street, grazing the corner of Holy Joe's house and showering the road with brickdust. Billy Staton, prancing about on the roof of his mother's car, heard the roar of an engine behind him and tried to turn round in mid-air. He missed his footing and fell down into the road, bouncing up on his feet again like a rubber ball. Petrified, he stared open-mouthed at the juggernaut bearing down on him.

With a shriek his mother came to her feet, snatched him up and threw herself into the house as the yellow dustcart roared by the front door making the whole house vibrate. There were those, years later, who would have said it was a pity Billy's mother was so quick and that it would have been a good thing if he'd been left in the road to be mown down by the council dustcart. It would have saved some people a lot of trouble.

Mr Rose Cottage brayed with insane laughter when everything before his eyes turned bright yellow as the dustcart thundered past just inches away from his window. In the kitchen behind him Mrs Rose Cottage uttered a heavy sigh and doubled the measure of rum she was adding to his morning cocoa. Dosing her husband with alcohol was the only way she knew to quieten his ravings and Dr Oakleigh said it could do little harm since the old fellow probably hadn't long to live, certainly not long enough to become an alcoholic.

In the Habenhowe house a second head was distending the orifice between Gladys Habenhowe's gaping thighs.

"Push!" the midwife commanded. "Come on, *push!*"

Gladys pushed. Sweat poured down her forehead and soaked the strands of carrot-coloured hair which straggled over her face, turning them dark brown. Suddenly she screamed. Then screamed again and gave birth for the second time that morning. Dr Oakleigh deftly tied off the second umbilical cord, cut it and passed the slippery new-born child to the midwife. He leaned over the exhausted woman on the bed.

"Twin girls, Mrs Habenhowe. Both fine."

She smiled weakly up at him, the sweat now condensing into droplets on her face. "Twins? Well, I never,"she said.

With considerable luck Stan had navigated his vehicle to the end of Ferry Street with only minor damage— mainly broken and sheared-off outside mirrors—to the cars parked there. The narrow right-angled turn to the left at the T-junction at the top of the street was another matter altogether, however.

Sid covered his face with his hands as Stan slewed the dustcart round in an impossible attempt to turn the corner. Stan stamped on the brakes and halted the vehicle with its front bumper jutting into the doorway of a house. He threw the gear into reverse, accelerated ... and rammed Wally Kronks's house on the corner behind him. The iron hood over the rear of the dustcart sliced into the brickwork, demolishing the corner pier and penetrating the upstairs front bedroom at floor level. But for the protection of this stout metal overhang the man riding the tailplate would have been squashed against the wall of the house like a fly.

Hauling on the steering wheel like a maniac, Stan drove forward again. As the roof of the vehicle tore free from the building, bringing down much of the front bedroom wall, it brought with it from the bedroom a small burden in a tartan pinafore dress. Stan slammed on the brakes once more, the bricks and debris tumbled off into the road and his unexpected passenger was propelled to the front end of the roof. With one further manoeuvre Stan cleared the right-angle between the houses and lurched forward again, totally unaware of the devastation he had caused.

"Told you I could do it, didn't I?" he bellowed proudly as they gathered speed again, sweeping away the hanging baskets of geraniums projecting from one of the houses.

Ferry Street was only single width where it emerged between the sides of two tall houses to join the top of the High Street. A row of overhanging trees lined the wall of Dr Oakleigh's house on the corner making the road into a tunnel at that point and reducing the headroom to little more than that of a car. The dustcart charged through the foliage like an elephant through the jungle and burst into the High Street festooned with leaves and twigs and covered with red geranium petals.

Stan swung the wheel to the right and pressed the accelerator to the floorboards. "Hold tight!" he shouted as they sped across the railway bridge and up the hill. "Soon be back now."

The phone was ringing for a second time in the small council house halfway up the hill where Tanniford's only policeman, Ted Jordan, lived and had his office. The first call, a few minutes ago, had come from old Hetty whose cottage backed on to the Spreadeagle. Hetty was always complaining about the goings-on in the pub especially at night. This morning she was complaining about the dustmen. "Incapable . . . blind drunk . . . falling down and rolling about in the road." Her voice whistled through the gaps in her teeth, quavering and distorted. Ted was puzzled as he listened to her. This wasn't like Sid and his lads.

Before he'd decided what to do the phone rang again. This time it was Dr Oakleigh's wife. He listened respectfully. Mrs Oakleigh wasn't one to exaggerate. She'd heard the commotion as the dustcart crashed its way round the corner by Wally Kronks's house and had looked out of her top window as it went past her house and plunged through the overhanging trees.

"You saw a *what* on the roof?" Ted asked, unable to believe his ears. "*A child?*"

"Yes!" Even a doctor's wife couldn't be expected to remain calm in the face of what she had seen. Her voice rose hysterically. "It's little Dolly Kronks. I recognise the dress."

At that moment a bright yellow mass flashed past in the road beyond Ted's front garden. His horrified gaze, alerted by Mrs Oakleigh's words took in the greenery, the geraniums and—. "Oh, God!" he breathed. There *was* a child, a little girl, her tartan dress flapping as she clung to the forward end of the roof behind the driving cab. He slammed down the phone. Then, swearing profusely in his agitation, he tore out of the house and jumped into his small white car standing in the yard. Headlights on, blue lamp flashing and siren screeching, he raced after the refuse cart.

The midwife watched Dr Oakleigh examining the after-birth. Then, wanting to show that she understood what he was doing, she said:

"There's only one placenta, isn't there, doctor? That means they're not fraternal twins. They're identical twins, aren't they?"

He nodded, preoccupied with his examiantion. "There is rather more to it than that with these two." A colleague of his—Dr Samuels—who made a special study of twins, would expect all the data he could give him on this case. The midwife thought she heard him utter a soft whistle of surprise. As she often said over the years: "I think Dr Oakleigh knew there was something special about those Habenhowe twins right from when they were born."

The policeman began to overhaul the dustcart as it approached Tanniford Cross. Stan and the other two men in the front were deaf to any sound but the thunder and clatter of their own vehicle. The man riding at the rear couldn't hear the approaching siren either as he swayed about hanging on to the grabrail and yodelling at the top of his voice.

As the dustmen careered round the bend at Tanniford Cross the extra passenger they had picked up from Wally Kronks's house was thrown off the roof and into the path of Ted Jordan's car. The policeman trod desperately on his brakes, burnt rubber from his tyres smoking on the tarmac as he squealed to a halt only inches short of the small, still, bundle. He was out of the car and kneeling beside it before his shocked brain caught up with his eyes. What was lying there untidily in the road, dress thrown up and exposing chubby pink thighs and white satin panties, was not a little girl but a life-sized doll. "One of those with human hair that speaks whole sentences and wets itself'" he explained to his wife in disgust later. "One of the sleeves had caught on a jagged bolthead on the leading edge of the roof so that it looked as though she was holding on with her hands. Mrs Kronks had put one of her little daughter's dresses on the doll which made Mrs Oakleigh think she was seeing Dolly Kronks herself clinging to the top of the dustcart."

Ted threw the doll into the back of the car, jumped into the driving seat and sped off in pursuit again. He caught up with Stan and his mates where the road became a dual carriageway. As he drew alongside, Stan beamed down at him.

"It's ol' Ted," he told the other two and lifted his hand from the wheel to give a cheery wave. This caused the dustcart to swerve across the road, nearly crushing the policeman's car against the offside kerb. Ted Jordan gritted his teeth and accelerated past. Then, not being equipped with a POLICE—STOP sign on his car, he put his hand out of the window and waved it up and down.

"What's the silly bugger doing?" Stan demanded.

"I think he wants us to stop," Sid said.

Stan jammed on the brakes and the heavy refuse cart skidded to a standstill in a haze of dust. Ted stopped his car, leapt out and ran towards them.

"Out!" he ordered. "All of you! Out!"

They climbed down and stood on the grass verge swaying and grinning amiably. The policeman went back to his car, opened the boot and returned carrying several plastic bags. He handed one to each of them.

"Take a breath, put the tube in your mouth and blow," he ordered. "Fill the bag."

Obligingly, they blew. Ted collected the bags, solemnly examining each in turn. They had all turned green.

"You're drunk!" he announced. "The lot of you. You're all drunk."

"Only Stan was driving though," one of them protested.

Ted pointed to the mechanism at the rear of the vehicle which crushed and pulped the refuse. "That's *machinery*," he proclaimed, "and it's an offence to be under the influence of alcohol whilst in charge of dangerous machinery. I'm taking you all in."

He returned to his car and reached for the radio-telephone. He needed assistance. "*How* many?" county control asked, disbelievingly. "What's been going on down there?"

It was a question Ted put to Stan. "Sid's birthday," Stan lisped. "We bin celebrating."

Ever afterwards in Tanniford that Tuesday was known as 'The day the dustmen got drunk and smashed up Ferry Street.'

It was also the day the Habenhowe twins were born. They would affect people in the village much more than four drunk dustmen had done.

TWO

There was only one road in and one road out of Tanniford and that was over the railway bridge the dustcart had driven across that Tuesday morning. The village, the old part of it that is, was cramped into a loop of land formed by a bend in the river. It was confined there by the railway line which, although it followed the general line of the river, ran straight across the bend from one side to the other. There was no bridge from the village to the opposite bank of the river although strangers often drove down to the quay at Tanniford expecting to find one. There was, in fact, another route out of Tanniford. It went past the Spreadeagle and the small shipyard on the edge of the village and led up and over a hill beneath which the railway line disappeared into a tunnel. This was Rivenhall Road. The road was unmade though and not suitable for vehicles and it led only to open country.

Strictly speaking, the houses above the railway bridge, where Ted Jordan lived, were also part of Tanniford. How-ever, the railway effectively divided the area into two communities: those who lived above the bridge and those who lived below it. The people who lived above the bridge—where most of the new houses had been built— were regarded as interlopers by the inhabitants of the old part of the village. The new residents, in return, looked upon their neighbours down the hill as quaint and living behind the times. Some things about them they found amusing. The name of their vicar, for instance, as listed in the Tanniford Tidings, the parish magazine: Richard B. Gaye.

The Reverend Richard Gaye, a tall, lanky man with spectacles, was aware of the amusement his name caused to some people and was annoyed by it. In his youth the word 'gay' had meant just that: happy, light-hearted, cheerful. No connection with homosexuality. He hoped none of his parishioners thought him 'gay' in the modern sense of the word. Certainly none of those gathered round the font at the christening of the Habenhowe twins thought so. The service had reached the point where the priest usually took the infant from the mother preparatory to sprinkling it with the sanctified water. To everyone's surprise Gladys passed him both twins together, wrapped in one bundle.

The week before, she had asked the vicar if he would christen them both at once.

"You mean literally at the same moment, Mrs Haben-howe?"

"Yes, please, vicar."

He had smiled indulgently. Gladys was a simple village girl. Or rather she wasn't a girl anymore, she was a middle-aged woman. Age, he feared, had not improved her intelligence.

"Quite out of the question," he told her firmly. "The service makes no provision for such a circumstance."

"Mr Mayfield said I should ask you," she said, with heavy emphasis.

"Oh ... I see." The Reverend Gaye chewed his lip. Perhaps Gladys wasn't so simple after all. Henry Mayfield regularly donated very large sums to the Restoration Fund for the repair of the church tower.

"He is to be godfather to the girls," she said casually.

That had taken the vicar aback. It had also settled the matter. He would have to devise something. He decided to compromise ... to modify the service slightly.

Now, as he arranged the bundle in his left arm, relieved to find that the two infants together weighed less than some lusty armfuls he'd had to cope with, he wondered why Mayfield and his wife were undertaking the role of godparents. True, Gladys's husband worked as a deck-hand on one of the fishing trawlers owned by Henry Mayfield. But that was hardly a good enough reason. He glanced sideways at Harry Habenhowe, a small, wiry man, almost hidden behind his large wife. The vicar sighed. Ah, well, it was none of his business. He turned his head to Mayfield and said:

"Name this chi—" He corrected himself. "—these children."

"Georgina and Georgette."

The Reverend Gaye leaned over the font, scooped up a handful of water with his right hand and hesitated, looking enquiringly at Gladys Habenhowe standing beside him. She stared back at him. Understanding dawned. Silently she mouthed the names, pointing first to one head and then to the other.

He nodded. "I baptize *thee* Georgina and *thee* Georgette," he intoned, tipping his hand and sprinkling the heads in the order Gladys had indicated, "in the Name of the Father and of the Son and of the Holy Ghost. Amen."

The twins, who until then had been peacefully dozing, came rudely awake as water poured over their heads and into their eyes. Two mouths opened simultaneously and four lungs filled with air. The howling they set up was impressive, considering their size. The priest struggled on with the service.

"We receive these children into the congregation of Christ's flock and do sign them . . ." He paused and drew a firm cross on each forehead in turn. Since he used his thumbnail to do this, not surprisingly the howling increased in volume and the Reverend Gaye had to shout to make his words heard.

In an aside to her husband Marjorie Mayfield said sourly, "They didn't receive the sign of the Cross too well, did they? Isn't that supposed to be a bad omen?"

"Don't talk like the villagers," he muttered.

"I *am* a villager!" she snapped. "Or at least I was before you married me."

"Well, it's superstitious clap-trap," he said in an angry whisper.

Marjorie Mayfield flicked an imaginary speck of dust from her velvet jacket with a gloved hand and said nothing. She was a thin, intense woman, not long past thirty and becoming bitter that nine years of marriage to Henry Mayfield had not resulted in children. The village thought she'd done well for herself snaring Henry Mayfield with his fleet of trawlers and his money; but Marjorie didn't think she'd been so lucky. She would have given the lot to experience the joy she'd seen in Gladys Habenhowe's face earlier as Gladys bent over the babies in their pram.

Like the vicar, she too wondered why her husband had agreed to be a godparent to the Habenhowe children.

When she'd asked him he'd said: "Harry Habenhowe has worked for me for years—and before him his father worked for my father. When Gladys asked me I could hardly refuse. It's a matter of good staff relations, my dear." Mrs Mayfield was not entirely convinced by this explanation but since she could think of no other reason for his action she accepted it.

As the vicar droned on Henry Mayfield glanced round the circle of people at the font and hoped that they too would believe he was being godfather to tte twins out of the goodness of his heart. Two of them knew it was not so, of course. Gladys herself and Carol Cole. He caught Gladys's eye. She smiled at him happily. He forced a faint smile in return.

She'd come to his house one day when his wife was out and made her demand quite blatantly. "I'm not young," she said. "Too old for babies, some would say. Harry and I have no relations worth speaking of—leastways none who would look after twins and I'd like to be sure my little ones'd be all right if anything should happen to me or Harry. I want you to be their godfather." She paused and smiled from one side of her mouth. "For Old Times' Sake, you might say. I helped *you* once, remember?"

"And a sorry mess that turned out, didn't it?" he retorted bitterly.

"That wasn't *my* fault. Now I want a favour from you. It isn't much to ask and the chances are you'll never have to do anything."

"But what would people say?" he protested. "They might think . . . well, that . . ." He trailed off.

"What—you and me?" She chuckled. "That'd be a lark, wouldn't it? Let them think what they like."

He clutched at another straw. "What about your husband?"

"He'll think you're doing it because you're a good employer who wants to be kind to his staff."

"I'm not sure I want to be that kind." He tried to outstare the hard blue eyes gazing at him from under a shock of ginger hair. They said Gladys Habenhowe had a wild temper when she was roused. He dropped his eyes again. She said harshly:

"I hear you're standing for county council this year. Expect to get in they tell me. Well, there's a thing or two people in Tanniford and the county might want to know about you, Henry Mayfield, before they vote."

"That's blackmail!"

"Maybe it is and maybe it isn't. I'm not asking for money. I simply want to protect my children's future. You could call it taking out insurance."

"Even if I agree to being their godfather that doesn't carry any legal obligations, you know."

"Carol will see to it that you take responsibility for them if the time comes," Gladys said confidently. "I've told her about our understanding."

"Understanding? We haven't reached any understanding."

"Oh yes we have. You'll do it," she said bluntly. "You'll do it because of what I know. The christening's Sunday week. Three-thirty at the church."

Because of the feeling of guilt that was always with him and because he dared not cross Gladys Habenhowe he'd agreed. Now, looking at the two infants in the vicar's arms, mewling and squalling, he hoped he would never have to be responsible for them. They looked ugly and troublesome. After Gladys's visit he'd consulted his accountant. Gladys's own words had given him the clue as to how to safeguard himself. He'd had the accountant arrange annuities and life insurance on Gladys and her husband with the twins and himself as co-beneficiaries.

Henry Mayfield's gaze shifted to Carol Cole standing with her husband and son on the other side of Harry Habenhowe. What a little raver she'd been at seventeen. She was still a good-looking girl but she has lost that ultra-slim figure and the boyish hips that had sent him crazy when she'd joined his office staff straight from school seven years ago.

He became aware that the Reverend Gaye's incantation was coming to an end and that the closing words were being directed at him. He hastily switched his attention to the vicar.

". . . and ye are to take care that these children be brought to the Bishop to be confirmed by him as soon as they can say the Creed, the Lord's Prayer and the Ten Commandments . . ."

The vicar concluded the service and restored the twins to their mother. In a jocular tone he said, "I do hope I had the names in the right order, Mrs Habenhowe."

"Oh yes, thank you, vicar, though I don't suppose it would matter so long as I know which is which."

"Er . . . no." The Reverend Gaye was still trying to decide what she meant as he moved away towards Dr Oakleigh. He'd been surprised to see the doctor and his wife among the group at the font.

"Not often we see you at a christening, doctor."

"No, but I delivered these two and a twin christening is rather unusual."

"Ah, a sort of double blessing you mean?"

More like a 'mixed blessing', the doctor thought, though he didn't say so. The morning after the twins were born he'd telephoned his colleague, Dr Samuels. "I have some data for your research project, David. I delivered twins in the village yesterday. They're definitely monozygotic."

"Good, good." Eagerly, Dr Samuels had taken down the medical details as Dr Oakleigh relayed them. He'd interrupted at one point. "One chorion and *one* amnion? Are you certain of that? It would be very, very rare. In fact I've only ever heard of one other case."

"I couldn't believe it myself so I double-checked. There is absolutely no doubt. It means the splitting of the cell into two occurred very late in the pregnancy, doesn't it?"

"So late it's a miracle they weren't conjoined like Siamese twins. Your Habenhowe twins are going to turn out even more alike than normal identical twins. In a sense they are a single personality with two identical bodies. Quite remarkable. Do you think the parents would co-operate in a study?"

"Not a chance, but I'll ask. If it hadn't been for the midwife I shouldn't even have attended the birth."

"You'll warn the parents of the problems, of course."

"I'll do my best. Unfortunately the mother doesn't believe in doctors."

"You must make her realise," Dr Samuels urged, "that there may be serious psychological difficulties ahead." He went on to suggest some of the troubles Mrs Habenhowe would face unless she heeded his advice. At the time Dr Oakleigh thought his colleague exaggerated.

One of Dr Samuels's prophecies—a minor one—came true at the christening. "A pound to a penny the parents choose alliterative names," he had said. "You know . . . Sally and Sarah, Molly and Mavis. They nearly always do."

Georgina and Georgette. He'd been right. Dr Oakleigh began to wonder if some of the other things Dr Samuels had foretold would also come true.

Mr Rose Cottage died three months later. Almost certainly Billy Staton hastened his end. After the incident of the dustcart Billy kept a careful ear open whenever he was playing about on his mother's car. He had nightmare memories of the day a great yellow monster had come roaring down the street and nearly flattened him. Of course, the refuse vehicle didn't come along Ferry Street ever again. The whole team had been suspended and then, after the court case, the men had been transferred to another area of the county.

Billy invented a new game which upset Mr Rose Cottage even more than the constant noises Billy sent booming along the street as he pounded his mother's car. The game consisted of standing in front of the window of Rose Cottage and making faces at the old man as he sat in his chair staring out. The first time Billy tried it—poking out his tongue and wiggling his fingers at the sides of his head—he was badly scared by the result. The old man reared up in his chair, his toothless gums opening and closing and his arms frantically waving. Billy ran away in terror. He couldn't resist the temptation to do it again, however, and then he discovered that the old man was chairbound and unable to raise himself up on his legs for more than a few seconds.

The only interest left in life to Mr Rose Cottage was to gaze out of the window and watch the street. It was all there was to his world.

"We haven't a telly, you see," his wife explained to the neighbours, "and that's his only entertainment. I don't know what he'd do without it."

Unfortunately for the old man, Billy's entertainment was to observe the effect of standing in front of the window making faces and blocking the view. At first he waited until Mrs Rose Cottage left on her morning round of the village shops. Then he found out that when she was home she stayed in the kitchen and took no notice of her husband's ravings. Billy played the game as often as he liked then. Ferry Street was more of a backwater than a street and there was seldom anyone watching. His father was away in the army and his mother, heavily pregnant, had no interest in what Billy did.

One day Billy hit upon a new idea. He took along a broom and swept it up and down the window-panes in front of the old man's eyes. Billy hopped around in glee as poor old Mr Rose Cottage threshed about in his chair more violently than ever, slavering and whinnying, before collapsing in a heap.

When Billy repeated the action the old man remained motionless, his bald head lolling on his chest. Billy stared in fascination at the thick hairs protruding from the nose and ears. He put his face against the glass, stuck out his tongue and made his favourite ugly face. There was no respone. He had finally done for Mr Rose Cottage. Disappointed, Billy slunk away, trailing the broom.

THREE

Gladys Habenhowe found that she acquired a new status in the village as the mother of twins. People who hadn't spoken to her in years stopped her in the street to enquire about the new arrivals. Gladys's sharp tongue had made her unpopular with the women of Tanniford but now everyone wanted to talk to her and she was pleased. Her husband was not pleased however. In the first place Harry hadn't wanted children at all, let alone two at once; and in the second place, if he *had* to have a child, he would have preferred a son.

"You look silly having a baby at your age," he told Gladys when she became pregnant.

"And who's made me look silly then?" she demanded. "Or do you think I somehow managed to do this on my own?"

"I thought you was barren," he muttered.

Later, after the babies were born he'd made the comment: "Don't know where *they've* come from. There's never been twins in my family nor yours before." He spoke accusingly as though the children might not be his.

"Don't you take that line with me, Harry Habenhowe," Gladys said sharply. "Anyways, identical twins don't run in families. That's the other sort—fraternal twins."

"Twins is twins," he said obstinately.

"That's just where you're wrong. The midwife explained it to me. Most twins are just two children who happen to be born at the same time because the eggs were fertilised together. Our two came from *one* egg. That means they're identical."

"Huh!" he snorted, peering at the two infants lying side by side. "Don't look much alike to me. One's bigger than the other for a start."

"That's Georgina," Gladys said confidently. "She was born first. She'll be the bossy one, midwife says. They'll grow more like each other as time goes on, you'll see."

"A death is always followed by a birth," Mrs Kronks told her husband at the funeral of Mr Rose Cottage. "There'll be another birth soon."

"There's bound to be," said Wally, who was a foreman at the shipyard and saw everything in terms of ships. "Molly Staton's down to her marks with that load she's carrying. She'll have to dock soon and drop her cargo."

Mrs Staton's 'cargo' was a baby girl whom she called Ruth. Someone had told her the name meant 'friend' and she felt badly in need of a friend. Her husband had been home on leave from the army. He was a violent, quarrelsome man and before his leave was up and he returned to barracks he'd given his wife a black eye and his son, Billy, a thrashing.

Billy hated the new addition to the family. The baby took all his mother's attention and he resented the way she fussed and fiddled with it for hours. Soon after the baby was born Billy began throwing his breakfast on the floor in the mornings. One morning his long-suffering mother locked the door and told him she wouldn't let him out of the house until he cleared up the mess. Billy went into a tantrum and hurled himself through the nearest window. Fortunately it was a sash window with the bottom half open. Billy picked himself up from the three-foot drop and ran up the street in his pyjamas screaming with rage. His eyes were screwed shut in temper and at the top of the street he crashed into the scaffolding outside Wally Kronks's house where workmen were repairing the damage done by the dustmen—the council having at last come round to putting the work in hand. Mrs Kronks dashed out from her house and tried to soothe Billy and received a pummelling from his flailing fists.

Dr Oakleigh's opportunity to offer Mrs Habenhowe some advice about the problems of bringing up twins came when she brought them to his surgery for their vaccinations. He was glad to see that if Gladys had no faith in doctors at least she believed in having her children immunised. It turned out that her beliefs were rather more complex than he realised.

"Well, there aren't any gasworks now, you see," she said by way of explanation.

"Gasworks?" He gaped at her.

Gladys, apparently, had a dread of whooping-cough which she'd contracted herself as a child. "I nearly died. Mum told me she used to wheel me round the gasworks every day in my pram. That's what saved me."

Dr Oakleigh's eyes glazed. "How?" he asked.

She smiled at him with her large, strong teeth. "You'd be too young to remember, doctor," she said sympathetically, as though youth was a kind of handicap, "but in those days they used to make gas from coal—Gas Light and Coke Company, see? Real smelly places gasworks were. There was one here in Tanniford—behind where the Spreadeagle is now. The doctor—he'd be long before your time—he told mum to take me there for an hour every day. The idea was that the strong fumes made you bring up the phlegm and that cured the whooping-cough. It worked for me."

"Did it really?" he said weakly.

"Yes, but it's all different now, isn't it? It's North Sea gas. So I thought my two had better have this vaccination stuff."

"Yes, I see." Dr Oakleigh prepared the vaccines and administered them wondering as he did so how to broach the subject he wanted to discuss with her. She provided the opening for him herself.

"Don't look quite the same yet, do they?" she said. There was a note of disappointment in her voice. Georgina's bald head showed fine reddish streaks. Georgette, the smaller child, had jet-black, baby-hair which had not yet rubbed off.

"They will do eventually," he assured her. "And that is something I'd like to talk to you about, Mrs Habenhowe."

He tried to impress upon her the importance of treating each child as an individual in its own right and warned her against encouraging or emphasising their sameness. Gladys, however, was unmoved and when he mentioned Dr Samuels's desire to make a study of Georgina and Georgette she bridled immediately.

"You make them sound like freaks!" she cried angrily. "They're my babies! Lovely little normal healthy babies. I don't need any doctor telling me how to bring up my own children!" Before he could pacify her she had snatched them up and stormed out of the surgery.

She had still been incensed when she was feeding them at home that evening. "Not treat you the same?" She clicked her tongue. "The idea! What does *he* know about it?" She pulled the bottle-teat from one mouth and placed it in the other. "There. You're going to share and share alike. You'll do everything together and you'll be the spitten image of each other. It's only natural."

By the time Georgina and Georgette were two years old Gladys had her wish: two little look-alikes; and she underlined their similarity by dressing them in exactly the same clothes and doing their hair the same. The twins had Gladys's carroty hair and pale complexion but not her angular features. Instead, their faces were rounded like their father's. They were slow in learning to talk—or rather in learning to talk to other people. For they communicated with each other easily enough, though in a form of baby-talk that Gladys found difficult to understand. For a while their adult vocabulary seemed to consist of two words only and they used them in response to every question.

"What's your name, dear?"

"I'm two."

"Where's your mummy?"

"I'm two."

Tanniford had its share of cuddle-hungry grannies and often one or other girl would be grabbed in the street and crushed against some strange bosom. "You little angel," the woman would coo. "Give us a kiss."

"I'm two!" the half-stifled infant would shout.

At first Gladys thought the twins were simply taking longer than other children to learn to say their words properly. As the months went by however, and they chattered more and more between themselves in a jabber that was incomprehensible to her, she became alarmed. The final straw came when her friend Carol Cole, who lived next door to her in North Street, said one day:

"Hughie was like that, you know, Gladys."

This caused Gladys to panic. Carol's boy, Hugh, was backward. He was nine years old but had the mentality of a child of four. She appeared in Dr Oakleigh's surgery that

evening together with Georgina and Georgette. She had
not visited the doctor since the time she'd stormed out of
his surgery three years ago and it was only with reluctance that she sought his advice now.

Dr Oakleigh listened patiently as Gladys explained her
worry. Georgina and Georgette stood doll-like beside her,
holding hands. He observed them curiously. They were
astonishingly alike and very solemn-looking. When
Gladys had finished he tried talking to them. They
answered him mostly in monosyllables. He compared
them with his son Robert at that age. Robert had been
bright and cheerful with a great deal to say for himself.
Yet the twins weren't lacking in intelligence as Gladys
feared. He was sure of that. Of course, he hadn't heard
them speaking the gibberish Gladys had described. Indeed
Georgina and Georgette had been oddly silent except
when he addressed them. They had not spoken between
themselves at all, he noticed.

"Do you think they understand each other when they
use this baby-talk you told me about?" he asked.

"Oh yes, I'm sure they do," she said. "It's just that none of
it makes sense to me."

"I suspect that they're developing a private language of
their own, Mrs Habenhowe. This happens sometimes with
twins. You see, they spend more time in each other's
company than with anyone else—including you. So it's
hardly surprising if they communicate better with one
another than with other people. I don't think you have
much to worry about. They will probably grow out of it. In
the meantime I should encourage them to mix with other
children more."

Gladys tried to follow the doctor's advice if only because
she disliked being excluded from her children's conversa-
tions. But Georgina and Georgette showed a marked
reluctance to play with any other children except Hugh
next door. And although their vocabulary gradually
increased until it was normal they continued talking to
each other in their own way, giggling and laughing, with
Gladys not understanding a word.

She didn't mind them playing with Hugh because the
three of them seemed to get on so well together and though

Hugh was a big, clumsy lad he was gentle and protective towards Georgina and Georgette. It annoyed her, though, that after a while he was able to follow some of the things they were saying when they lapsed into their private talk whereas she and Carol couldn't.

By the age of five the twins had devised their own response to the question they were to suffer all their lives.

"Which are you—Georgina or Georgette?" someone would demand, poking one of them in the chest.

"She's Georgie," the other twin would answer.

"Oh? And what are *you* called?"

This time the first girl would reply. "She's Georgie too."

Often the questioner would persist with: "You can't both be called Georgie," and they would chorus, "Yes we can!" and scamper away shouting with laughter.

Some people found this amusing; others were angry. One or two, including Dr Oakleigh, became thoughtful, realising the Habenhowe twins had erected another barrier between themselves and the rest of the world.

Molly Staton was relieved when Billy suddenly became less hostile to Ruth when she was about four years old. He was then eight and Mrs Staton was touched by the way Billy would take his little sister by the hand and lead her off to play. What she didn't know was that Ruth had become the leading character in the game Billy played with Robert Oakleigh, the doctor's son.

In a corner of the churcyard stood a holly tree which had been growing steadily higher and wider for years. On the exposed side its evergreen leaves formed a thick screen down to the ground. Behind this screen, between the base of the tree and the enclosed corner of the high brick wall behind it, was an area, hidden from view, which made an ideal spot for children to play. It was here that Billy played 'hospitals' with Robert and Ruth. The 'hospital' comprised cardboard boxes from the grocer's and two packing cases dragged up from the shipyard.

Ruth was always the patient. Robert, although a year younger than Billy, was the doctor. "My father's a doctor and I know what to do," Robert had said. "So either you let me be the doctor or I don't play." Billy was content with the arrangement. He gave the orders and stood and watched; and he experienced a strange new excitement watching Robert and his sister.

Whichever way the game was played and whatever was supposed to be Ruth's ailment, there invariably came a point at which she had to be undressed. Billy insisted on being the nurse and performing this function himself. Ruth didn't object. In fact she rather enjoyed her brother's interest in her after he'd refused to play with her for so long. Nor did she mind Robert 'operating' on her. His hands were soft and gentle and she liked him. She didn't believe him though, the time she was supposed to be having a baby. It was plain daft to say it came out of *there*, even if his dad was a doctor.

Then one day the trio found they had an audience. The Habenhowe twins appeared with Hugh Cole in tow and stood solemnly watching as Ruth was put through her daily inspection for injuries and illnesses. Billy decided that her leg needed cutting off for a start. Everyone watched in fascination as Robert went through a convincing mime of a surgeon preparing for and then carrying out an operation. As he sawed at Ruth's thigh with a ruler she groaned realistically.

"Don't be silly," Robert said sharply. "You've had an injection and you can't feel anything, so be quiet."

Obediently, Ruth stopped groaning. However, when that part was over she declined to be undressed for the usual 'further examination'. Faced with a strange audience she had suddenly become shy.

"Him! Him!" she squeaked, pointing to Hughie. "He wants the doctor. Then I can be the nurse."

Hughie, now twelve years old and tall with it, grinned amiably.

"Come on, Lofty," urged Billy, who had had a sudden inspiration as to where this could lead, "it's good fun."

Hughie stepped forward eagerly, more than willing to co-operate. The village children seldom let him join in their games. He lay down on the packing cases.

"What is the matter with you?" asked Robert.

Hughie pondered, his slow brain wrestling with the problem. "Pain in me belly," he suggested at last. He smiled happily and allowed himself to be exposed and prodded without protest. The twins moved closer, gravely observing the proceedings. Robert, who was keen to follow in his father's footsteps, had picked up the general idea of how things were done from watching television pro grammes and Hughie was duly cut open and stitched up again.

As Hughie climbed off the packing cases Billy pointed at the twins. "Now it's your turn," he said. The idea had come to him at the moment Hughie had agreed to play. He reckoned that Hughie would become an ally after he'd been through the ordeal himself and that two five-year-old girls would be no match for three boys. Their pale faces stared at him.

"Come on! You have to be examined." Billy felt a stab of pleasure at the thought of forcing them to do what he wanted.

They shook their heads. "No," they answered together.

Billy seized one of them by the arm. "You have to let the doctor look at you," he insisted, dragging her towards the packing cases. The other girl hung on to her sister's arm trying to hold her back. Suddenly Billy was enfolded from behind in a bear-like hug that squeezed the breath from him and obliged him to release his captive.

"She don't want to. Leave her be," Hughie said against his ear.

"Lemme go!" Billy snarled, kicking furiously and sur prised to find that he was helpless in Hugh Cole's iron grasp.

"*I* know what," piped Ruth. "Let's take *Billy* to hospital."

"Yes, it's time he had a turn," Robert agreed. He was angry with Billy for bullying a girl.

Shouting and spitting, Billy Staton was spreadeagled on the packing cases. Hughie immobilised his top half by sitting on his chest and the twins each clung on to a leg. With swift, deft movements Robert exposed his new patient's middle section to view. Billy raved and swore with humilitation.

"Aha! All this needs cutting off," said Robert sternly, pretending to saw at Billy's appendages with a ruler.

At this Billy's temper burst into uncontrolled fury.

Heaving violently, he began to break free. Finding they were no longer able to hold him the children scattered and fled.

"I'll get you!" Billy screamed after them. "I'll kill you! All of you! You see if I don't!"

It was a very long time before Billy Staton played behind the holly tree again; and when he did he was a young man and it was not a game.

FOUR

One outcome of the incident in the churchyard was that
Robert Oakleigh stopped playing with Billy and became
friendly with Hugh Cole and the Habenhowe twins. His
mother was not altogether happy about this. She didn't
mind when the four children played in her own garden and
she could keep an eye on them but she disliked it when
Robert was down in North Street.

"It's the Cole boy I'm worried about," Mrs Oakleigh
explained to her husband. "He's twelve and he's a big boy
for his age. He shouldn't be playing with Robert or with
those little girls. They're too young for him."

"There's nothing to worry about," Dr Oakleigh assured
her. "Hughie Cole is backward, poor lad, but he's quite
harmless and there's certainly no violence in him. Believe
me, the children are safer with him than they would be
with some of the other village children."

Gladys was relieved that Georgina and Georgette had
another friend besides Hugh although she wasn't too
pleased that he was the doctor's son. She thought Robert
might carry tales to his father about her and her offspring.
Gladys didn't want anyone to know—least of all Dr
Oakleigh, whose advice on the subject she had spurned—
that she was beginning to have difficulty in distinguishing
between Georgina and Georgette. At first she had only
been in doubt if she was speaking to one girl and the other
one happened to be out of sight. She'd always known which
was which as soon as she saw them together. Lately, however, she'd had to admit to herself that she was no longer
always certain of telling one from the other even when
they were standing side by side.

When they were about six months old, and beginning to
confuse her, she'd adopted simple precautions to make
sure she didn't mix them up. She'd sewn name-tags into
their clothes and put coloured bracelets on their wrists;
and she'd taken care not to have them both naked at the
same time unless they had their bracelets on. Once they
started to talk and could say their names she had assumed
that was the end of her problem and had stopped worrying.

It had not entered her mind that the children themselves might choose to deceive her. The shock had come one evening in the summer, shortly after their fifth birthday.

It had been one of those sweltering evenings when it was difficult to sleep because of the heat. Gladys heard the twins moving about and talking after she had put them to bed. She had gone upstairs to see what they were doing and when she entered their bedroom she found the two girls sitting on the floor. Both were naked.

Gently Gladys chided them. "I know it's very hot, my loves, but it'll turn cool in the night. Now, put your nighties on and—" She stopped. On the floor in front of them were their bracelets.

"What are those doing there?" she demanded. "You know you mustn't take your bracelets off. Put them on at once!" They stared at her without moving and she felt a spasm of alarm.

"Put them on!" she repeated. She picked up the bracelets and held them out. One was red and one was blue. They were engraved with the girls' names though Georgina and Georgette had been able to tell their own bracelet by the colour long before they could read their names. Flabbergasted, Gladys watched as one girl took the bracelets and slipped both of them on her wrist. Angrily Gladys bent down and snatched them off again. She held out the blue one which was Georgina's.

"Georgina?" There was no answer. She changed the question to a command. "Georgina! Put this on at once!" She glared at them, confident that one of them would respond. Instead they looked at each other and giggled. Her temper rising, Gladys stepped forward intent on delivering a smacking. She stayed her hand however as Georgina and Georgette threw their arms round one another and huddled together. Punishment would solve nothing. She pretended to laugh.

"I *see* . . . this is a lovely new game, is it? Well, it's very late and it's time for bye-byes now. Mummy wants to kiss you goodnight. Georgette first. Which is Georgette?" She knelt on the floor and leaned towards them. There was an agonising wait for her until a small voice said: "I'm Georgette, mummy."

In a rush of relief Gladys gathered the children in her arms and kissed them. She put their nightdresses back on and tucked them into bed. As she stooped over the bed to kiss them a second time Georgina asked: "Didn't you *really* know which was me, mummy?"

Gladys hesitated. The truth, or a lie? She forced a smile. "Yes, of course I knew. Mummy was just pretending," she said. She was disconcerted when Georgina turned to Georgette and spoke to her in words that Gladys couldn't understand. "Stop that!" she said sharply. Georgina looked at her sulkily. "What were you saying to Georgette?" Gladys demanded.

It was Georgette who answered. "Georgina said she's tired and wants to go to sleep."

Gladys regarded them doubtfully. She wished her husband, Harry, were here instead of away with the trawler fleet. Although he took very little interest in his daughters she could probably have persuaded him to give them a good talking to. Except, Gladys admitted to herself, she wasn't too sure what she wanted him to say. The girls were displaying an independence of will that she could scarcely credit and it wasn't to her liking. Gladys had heeded her own mother in everything and had obeyed her implicitly almost to the day she married; her father would have warmed her backside for her if she hadn't. Yet, instinctively, Gladys knew that it would serve no purpose to beat Georgina and Georgette. That would only drive them closer together and further away from her.

In the autumn of that year there was a launching at Tanniford shipyard. On average a ship was launched every eighteen months. The yard built small coasting vessels, mainly for British shipowners, but occasionally there would be an order from Denmark or Holland. Several times over the years the shadow of nationalisation had fallen across the shipyard, but so far it had managed to escape public ownership. During the Second World War fast MTBs for the Royal Navy had been built there but even then the yard remained in private hands.

Tanniford shipyard was unlike any other shipyard in the country. Visitors to the village—and Tanniford, with its Norman church and quaint narrow streets, attracted

visitors—invariably halted in shock when they first encountered the shipyard. Usually they had wandered along
Spring Street or down Ferry Street and past the Black Dog
until they came to a tall building beside the river. Beyond
this building, which was clad with sheets of corrugated
iron, they expected to come to open fields. There were open
fields there all right but what people didn't expect to find,
as they rounded the corner of the building, was that the
nearest field had been concreted over and that towering
above them was the skeleton of a two-thousand-ton ship.
Around this concrete apron oxyacetylene cutters and
welders would be at work assisted by three overhead
cranes which lifted the heavy metal plates and the completed sections into place on the hull. Sheets of thick steel
were stored upright around the field and the ground was
littered with the metal offcuts from bulkhead doors and
portholes which gave the place the appearance, at first
sight, of a vast timber yard.

Ever since her husband became a councillor Marjorie
Mayfield had longed to launch a ship from the Tanniford
shipyard and she had nagged Henry Mayfield solidly
about it.

"I don't see why you can't just ask one of the directors,"
she said.

"It's not up to the yard directors, Marjorie. It's the shipowners who decide."

"Well, at least *try*," she urged.

After a long time and much lobbying it was eventually
arranged that Councillor Mayfield would make a speech at
the next launching and that his wife would name the ship.
It was a proud moment for Henry Mayfield as he mounted
the rostrum with his wife that autumn day. Marjorie was
wearing a magenta dress and coat. She had bought the
clothes especially for the occasion and she had been particularly careful about the colour. A few weeks before the
ceremony she had asked him what colour the vessel was
painted.

"What the devil does that matter?"

"I don't want my outfit to clash."

As he looked up now at the high, silver-grey bow of the
ship it seemed a long way away from them. Marjorie could

have worn any colour, he thought.

The day was cool but sunny and as he drew the notes for his speech from his pocket Henry Mayfield was well content. This would be an enjoyable event, one to remember. He gazed down on the expectant faces below him, knowing practically all of them. Near the foot of the rostrum he spotted a journalist and photographer from the local paper. A launching was a big occasion in Tanniford. Most of the village were there and all the shipyard workers and their families. The children had a day off from school and the three pubs—the Spreadeagle, the Black Dog and the Anchor—were open all day.

Councillor Mayfield adjusted the microphone and commenced his speech. He had taken considerable pains over the preparation. He began with a potted history of shipbuilding in Tanniford which dated back to the 1700s. It was to be a long speech.

"*Too* flaming long," Wally Kronks growled as Mayfield went on and on. "We'll have passed the top of the tide soon."

As yard foreman, Wally was responsible for the actual launching into the water. It was he who had laid out the king-sized baulks of timber on which the keel rested. His eye alone that lined them up, decided on the slope to the water and where they were placed; and it was his calculation that had fixed the exact point of time in the tide's rise at which the vessel should take to the water. All of this was second nature to Wally. He'd been doing it for fifteen years and his father for a lifetime before him.

The children in the crowd became restless as Councillor Mayfield droned on. They were only interested in seeing the big vessel plunge into the water and the great splash that followed.

Hugh Cole sauntered off along one side of the hull to where his stepfather was standing, mallet in hand, awaiting the signal from Wally to knock away the dog-shores—heavy blocks of timber that held the vessel steady and prevented her sliding down the launching ways and into the water. The Habenhowe twins followed him. Lionel Cole took no notice of the children behind him. His eye was on the foreman a hundred feet away under the bow of the

vessel. He didn't see Georgina and Georgette wander
forward below the V-shaped bottom of the hull. The village
children often played in the shipyard in the evenings when
work had finished and the two girls had no fear of the steel
monster above them as they walked beneath the keel.
They had dodged in and out of the timbers and debris lying
there many times before. A waterman near the stern saw
them.

"Come out of there at once you little fools!" he shouted.
"She's going in at any moment."

Georgina and Georgette ran from under the keel and
stood hand in hand on the other side of the vessel from
Hugh and his stepfather. The waterman quickly assessed
their position. They were on the wrong side and on their
own but they were safe where they were and there was no
time for them to move back.

"Stay there and don't move!" he ordered.

Suddenly everything happened at once. Wally Kronks
at the bow had been making frantic signals to one of the
directors who was standing behind Councillor Mayfield.
The man at the water's edge who had watched the tide
move slowly up the concrete slip under the stern of the
vessel had given Wally a sign with his hand. The tide had
changed and had already dropped a foot. Ships at Tanniford were put in during the fortnightly highwater springs
when the tides were highest. This was also the time when
the tide ran out the fastest, of course. If there was not
enough water under the stern of the vessel to support her
weight as she entered the water then instead of floating off
she would grind to a halt on the slip half in and half out of
the water like a beached whale. If, on the other hand, the
tide was too high then when the stern hit the water the
strain on the bow—still on the launching ways—became
intolerable and the hull could split at the seams. The
whole launching operation was extremely time-critical.

A gravelly voice in Councillor Mayfield's ear urged him
to finish speaking, ". . . else there'll *be* no ruddy launching!" Mayfield gabbled some closing words then turned to
his wife and called on her to name the ship.

"And be sharp about it!" someone hissed as she moved to
the microphone.

Mrs Mayfield was not to be hurried, however. It was not every day one launched a ship. She had bought an expensive new outfit. She had told all her friends about the event; and she had arranged for plenty of photographs to be taken of her casting the bottle of champagne against the bow. She had no intention of rushing these glorious moments. She would take her time.

Time had run out for Wally Kronks though. His arms were already extended outwards, alerting the men at the stern, as Marjorie Mayfield's voice floated through the public-address system and across the yard. She had practised long and hard to achieve the exact tone and modulation she so much admired in the voices of the Royalty and some other women in public life.

"I name this ship . . ." she began, speaking slowly and carefully. It was enough for Wally. If the bottle didn't break first time he would use the trip line to pitch the bottle against the side of the ship until it did break. He scissored his arms back and forth across his chest and the men by the water knocked away the wedges under the stern and pulled away the cradles and supports.

". . . *Alacrity*—" continued Mrs Mayfield and broke off in surprise as the bow in front of her suddenly lifted slightly. Down below her Wally raised his arms above his head in a wide V which was the final signal to the men on either side. Lionel Cole stepped forward with his mallet and knocked away the dog-shore on his side.

". . . may God bless her and all who sail in her," Mrs Mayfield concluded hurriedly and, swinging the bottle on its line, she hurled it at the already retreating bow. The bottle burst against the hull, champagne flowed over the new paintwork and the crowd cheered and applauded. Suddenly, the cheers turned to horrified gasps.

In the discussion and arguments that followed there were those who said that Wally was in such a panic that he went straight from one signal to the other without pause and that the side supports were knocked away too soon making the hull unstable even before it started to move. Others swore he'd signalled the starboard dog-shore away first. Whatever the cause, instead of moving majestically with gently increasing momentum down the launching ways and into the water, the ship began to slide sideways as well as downwards. In a matter of moments the hull would come right off the launching ways and topple to one side on its bilges.

There was a sudden cry from the centre of the crowd. "*My children!*" Gladys shrieked. The twins stood rooted to the ground in terror as the mammoth hull moved in their direction. "*Do something!*" Gladys screamed at Lionel Cole who was nearest to them although on the other side of the vessel. "*Save them!*" He lifted his hands in a gesture of helplessness. Men were scattering for their lives in all directions.

Then, from behind, someone flashed past him. Like an arrow Hugh Cole sped between the remaining blocks beneath the moving keel and came out on the other side— by some miracle avoiding the obstacles and falling timbers. Running madly, he extended his arms, aeroplane fashion, swept up the twins under each arm and hurtled onwards to crash on the ground in safety some twenty yards on. Behind him timbers splintered and king-sized blocks were smashed as the keel ground everything in its path to firewood.

Seconds later the turn of the bilge crashed down on the spot where the twins had been standing, cracking and powdering the concrete as though it had been the icing on a cake.

FIVE

For several moments there was a stunned silence after the *Alacrity* came to rest. She lay over on her starboard side, her stern lapped by the receding tide, a pathetic sight to the shipyard workers who had built her.

Hugh scrambled up and set Georgina and Georgette on their feet. The crowd sighed with relief as they saw them. The tragedy could have been much worse. People began running towards the trio. Hughie regarded the figures bearing down on him with alarm and had the twins not hung on to him he would have fled. The world was a bewildering place to Hughie. Most of the time people either ignored him or grumbled at what he did. Hardly anyone except his mother ever praised him. Now, to his amazement, he was surrounded by people who patted him on the back, shook his hand and even, in the case of Mrs Habenhowe, kissed and hugged him. His puzzled face cleared and broke into a wide grin.

The crowd around him fell back respectfully as Councillor Mayfield approached. He ruffled Hugh's hair and put an arm round his shoulders.

"That was a very brave thing you did, my lad," he said, his voice husky with emotion. He caught sight of the boy's stepfather on the edge of the crowd looking at him cold-faced and dropped his arm quickly. "Would you like to come up to my house for a while, Hughie? We're having a little party to celebrate the launching and . . ." He tailed off. "Well, it won't be a celebration now," he went on, "but there's no sense in wasting the food and drink."

Hugh wasn't sure what a celebration was, but he understood food and drink well enough. He nodded eagerly.

"Right, I'll fix it with your dad." Mayfield walked over to where Cole was standing. "Mind if Hughie comes up to my place with the others, Cole? I'd like the directors to meet him. And that reporter wants to talk to him too."

Cole shrugged his shoulders, contemptuously. "Suit yourself. It makes no odds to me."

Mayfield stared at him. He wondered what kind of a stepfather Cole was to the boy. Did having Carol in his bed every night compensate for bringing up her backward son?

"The boy saved those girls' lives. What he did was remarkable . . . especially for him," he said.

"You don't imagine he thought it out, do you?" Cole said harshly. "It was blind instinct. He's soppy about those Habenhowe kids. When their mother started shouting he just ran. He didn't *think*. He's not capable of thinking."

"He showed tremendous courage!" Mayfield said fiercely. "You should be proud of him. I know that Carol—" He checked himself. "I'm sure his mother will be." He turned abruptly and walked away.

The representative of Lloyd's underwriters who attended the launching took control of the situation down by the waterside. The vessel had come under Lloyd's juris diction as soon as the launch went wrong. Curious villagers were shooed away and a wide area around the *Alacrity* was roped off and marked with warning notices. The ship was no longer the property of the shipowners or the builders. It was now for Lloyd's to decide what was to be done.

Most of the crowd drifted away but some people stood for a long time gazing at the stranded ship. Nothing like this had happened before, at least not within their memories. The last drama had been five years ago when the drag chains had parted as the ship entered the water and she had surged across the river and embedded her stern in the mud on the opposite bank. No harm had been done and she had floated off with the next tide. Today was a different matter altogether.

In the village pubs trade was brisk. Business was always good on the day a ship was launched. Today it reached record levels as the arguments raged and the discussions lengthened. It was thirsty work.

In the Spreadeagle, which was the welders' favourite haunt, they blamed the disaster on the watermen. Their calculations were up the creek. The launching ways were crooked. The tide was wrong. They had panicked. It was all their fault.

Over in the Black Dog, Wally Kronks himself laid the blame squarely on the designers. "They were bringing in modifications all the time we was building her. They altered the centre of gravity without knowing, that's what. She would never have slewed like that otherwise."

The general opinion in the Anchor, which was on the quayside and where the watermen gathered, was that Wally Kronks had 'lost his eye' and that he hadn't set out the keel blocks correctly. One man maintained that Wally had been drunk at the time. "Pissed as a newt, he was." Another man thought the wood used to make the dog-shores had been suspect. "Years old it was. Rotten as a pear. I told him so but he wouldn't listen." A third man reckoned the tide had dropped too far. "That berk Mayfield was beating his gums for too long. Wally should have called off the launch."

In the Mayfield house at the top of the hill leading out of Tanniford the atmosphere was subdued as the guests sipped their wine and nibbled the food. The discussions and allegations here were more restrained since only one or two of them knew anything about the technicalities of launching a ship. Mayfield Hall—an earlier Mayfield had actually named it that—was a large, early-Victorian house standing in an acre of land. It was double-fronted with steps leading up to the front door. At the foot of the steps, on the coping pieces either side, sat two ornamental lions. Their haunches and rumps were defaced with initials and marks that had been scored into them by children during the fetes and jumble sales that took place in the grounds. Mayfield Hall was the recognised venue in Tanniford for open-air events of that nature.

In the long drawing-room that ran the full depth of the house on one side, Councillor Mayfield did his best to cheer up his guests. As he circulated among them he made a joke of the affair.

"Some launching, eh? Marjorie put the mockers on that tub all right, didn't she?"

Once, his wife heard him and gave him a savage look. She was talking to the vicar who was trying hard to comfort her and to convince her that the mishap was not an ill-omen to bring bad luck on the *Alacrity* and those who would eventually sail in her.

"Really, Mrs Mayfield," he said a trifle impatiently, "you must have a little more faith in Our Lord than that.

Just think of the miracle of young Hugh Cole today. Did you not see the Divine Hand at work there?"

Marjorie Mayfield looked at Hugh who was standing at one of the buffet tables shovelling ice-cream into his mouth as fast as he could. "Yes, truly that was a miracle," she agreed. She gave a shudder at the thought of how she would have felt if she'd launched a ship that had crushed two little girls to death. She brightened. "You're such a comfort, vicar."

Dr Oakleigh also was watching Hugh at the ice-cream and marvelling at his capacity. He'd often wondered about Hugh Cole. Not about his backwardness because he understood that. He'd referred the boy to a psychiatrist paediatrician when the mother had come to him for advice some years ago. The lad was feeble-minded and always would be. Unhappily there was nothing to be done for him.

What intrigued Dr Oakleigh was why Carol Cole should have apparently felt in some way responsible for her son's condition. Before he was born, Carol—then a pretty teenager—had worked in the Mayfield offices on the quay. She'd lived with her parents in North Street next door to the Habenhowes. One day, without warning, the family had moved to another part of the county. A year later Carol had returned with six-months-old Hugh. Almost at once she'd married Lionel Cole, a melancholy, hard-faced man who worked in the shipyard. After the wedding they took up residence in the house in North Street. It had been unoccupied ever since Carol's family had left. All the weatherboard houses in North Street belonged to the Mayfield firm and why the house should have been allowed to remain empty for a year without re-letting was something of a mystery.

Carol's parents hadn't attended the wedding. Nor had they visited her since. It was rumoured in the village that they would have nothing more to do with their daughter. Lionel Cole had not been responsible for Carol's pregnancy. He made that clear from the beginning by always referring to Hugh as 'my stepson'. Ironically, Hugh bore some resemblance to his stepfather. He was tall and strongly-built like Lionel and he had the same fair, straight hair. Unlike his stepfather, however, he was happy and constantly smiling.

Dr Oakleigh decided it was time for him and his wife to slip away from Mayfield's party. He didn't enjoy these gatherings but, like the vicar, his position in the community required him to accept invitations to them. He sauntered into the hall looking for his wife to ask her if she was ready to leave. Mayfield suddenly appeared at his elbow having apparently followed him out.

"There's something I'd like to ask you, doctor," he said. "Would you come into the study a moment." He indicated a door at the end of the hall.

"Is this professional or private?" Dr Oakleigh asked warily. He was used to being asked for medical advice on social occasions. He met all such requests with a brisk, stock answer: "Come and see me at surgery."

His host laughed nervously. "No, it's not about me, or my health. It's not really about illness at all." He led the doctor into his study and closed the door.

"Go on," said the doctor, still wary. People adopted all kinds of subterfuges. Sometimes they pretended they were speaking about another person when in fact they were describing their own symptoms.

"Suppose—just suppose—a girl took a drug to abort herself and it didn't work. Could it damage the foetus?"

"With abortion pretty well on demand these days," Dr Oakleigh said tartly, "no girl needs to take a foolish risk like that."

Mayfield moved to the window and gazed out. "I wasn't thinking of these days," he said quietly.

A warning bell rang in Dr Oakleigh's head. "What you're talking about is a criminal offence," he said stiffly. "I don't care to discuss it." He moved to open the door.

Mayfield turned back from the window. The doctor paused with his hand on the doorknob, surprised by the haunted look on Mayfield's face. What on earth had come over the man?

"I have to know," Mayfield said hoarsely. "It's been worrying me for years."

Dr Oakleigh relented. He released the doorhandle. "What kind of drug?"

"Ergometrine."

Dr Oakleigh nodded. This was one of those old wives tales he'd encountered in his student days. Ergometrine caused contractions in the uterus—which was how the idea that it could cause an abortion had gained credence. Back-street quacks had once made fortunes out of selling the pills at outrageous prices to girls who were desperate to terminte their pregnancy.

"How big a dose?"

"Three or four pills I think."

Dr Oakleigh gave a half-smile and shook his head. "No effect at all—except perhaps as a laxative."

Mayfield's face cleared. "You're quite sure?" he asked eagerly. "Not even later, after the child was born? It couldn't . . . well, affect the brain for instance?"

In his mind Dr Oakleigh began making rapid connections. Hugh Cole? Mayfield seemed to have been unusually affected by the boy's rescue attempt in the shipyard and Dr Oakleigh had heard him repeatedly mentioning it when speaking to the guests. He noticed also that Mayfield's eyes softened when they rested on Hugh. It was then that he made another connection. Hugh's mother, Carol, at seventeen. Vivacious . . . attractive . . . working in Mayfield's office. Certain rumours. Good God! The man had been punishing himself ever since . . . riddled with guilt that he and Carol were responsible for Hugh being mentally retarded. Dr Oakleigh didn't care much for Mayfield but no man deserved to be saddled with a guilt like that for the rest of his life. Choosing his words carefully he said:

"In a particular case I can think of, the child's brain damage almost certainly came about through lack of oxygen during delivery at birth. Unfortunately that can happen sometimes with a home birth and an inexperienced midwife. The backwardness in that child had nothing whatever to do with any attempt at abortion."

He watched the relief flood into Mayfield's face and realised that his suppositions had been correct. He turned away, embarrassed by the tears appearing in Mayfields's eyes and went out of the door.

The attempt to float off the *Alacrity* from where she lay at the edge of the river was made a fortnight later on the next spring tide. The villagers awoke one morning to see a strange new sight dominating the skyline. "Biggest floating crane in the world," someone said. "They brought it all the way from Southampton."

That morning, two hours before high tide, the vast platform carrying the crane was in position in the middle of the river. A large canvas sling was put under *Alacrity's* stern—"like a nappy round a baby's arse," one wag described it—and chains were passed under it and hooked to the arms of the floating crane. Steel hawsers were attached to *Alacrity* and winched in hard aboard the flat, barge-like vessel on which the crane was mounted. Then everyone waited as the tide slowly approached high water.

The village had turned out in force to witness the spectacle. People had stationed themselves along the river bank hours beforehand and were squatting on the grass with their sandwiches and bottles of beer, observing the preparations. There was something of a carnival air about the proceedings and bets were being laid freely on the outcome, or rather on two outcomes: "She will", "She won't", according to whether the salvage operation was successful or unsuccessful. The watermen had bet heavily "She won't". The welders had put their money on "She will." The rest of the village had been about evenly divided.

At the internal enquiry that had taken place in the fortnight since the abortive launch the conclusion had been reached that no one factor was entirely to blame for the fiasco. Yes, the starboard dog-shores had collapsed due to faulty timber. Yes, the launching should have taken place at least fifteen minutes earlier and yes, in the hurry, the foreman's signals were misunderstood. Not one of these faults, on its own, would have mattered. Put them together though, and they were a recipe for disaster.

As the tide rose, tension among the onlookers mounted. The crane crew made last minute adjustments to the chains and cables. Winch engines were started and there was a fever of late betting amont the crowd. Children had stuck wooden sticks in the mud of the river bank, keeping a close eye on the rising water. Suddenly the main engines on the crane-barge whined and all eyes turned to the *Alacrity* lying like a wounded animal on the slipway with the water now lapping her amidships. The steel hawsers attached to her stern became bar-taut as the floating platform went astern. The chains tightened under *Alacrity's* stern and there was a slight upwards movement as the crane began its hoist. The movement was greeted by a loud "Aahh" from the watching crowd. There was no further movement however, and the floating crane and *Alacrity* remained frozen into a still picture.

"Tide's changed," someone called, who'd been observing the marker-sticks in the mud.

"They've had it now," said one of the watermen. His voice had a satisfied ring. He'd bet heavily that the salvage men wouldn't be able to lift *Alacrity* off.

All at once the water under the crane's floating platform boiled as all four engines screamed to full power and went hard astern. Still there was no movement or change in the position of *Alacrity* or the platform. A wire hawser snapped like cotton and snaked across the water with a hiss. Anyone in its path would have been decapitated. The crowd sighed, believing the struggle was lost. A moment later there was an almost imperceptible movement of *Alacrity's* stern. Everyone held their breath. Then slowly, very slowly, the ship was drawn into the water. There was a loud cheer from the onlookers. *Alacrity* was upright and in her true element at last.

Some months later, when the *Alacrity* had been fitted-out and commissioned, Harry Habenhowe decided he'd had enough of the bleak conditions on a fishing trawler and that, approaching fifty years of age, he deserved a more comfortable job. He signed on as deck-hand on the *Alacrity*.

Perhaps, despite the vicar's assurance to Marjorie Mayfield, there was something in the superstition about a bad launching. One wild March night, on *Alacrity's* maiden voyage, Harry Habenhowe was swept overboard and drowned.

SIX

Gladys Habenhowe mourned the death of her husband respectfully but not deeply. There had never been anything remotely approaching passion between them and all the while they'd been married he'd been away at sea for most of the time. So that when he was lost to the sea forever she hardly missed him. Their father's death had no great effect on Georgina and Georgette either. They too, had seen very little of him and what they had seen had left no impression on them.

When Henry Mayfield learned of Harry's death he made a hurried check of the life policies he'd taken out on him and was relieved to find that Gladys and her daughters would be well provided for. In fact they were going to be better off than if poor Harry had gone on living, he found. For a brief time he toyed with the idea of taking the family under his wing and becoming a father to the girls. Henry Mayfield had a penchant for little girls but he preferred them to be plump and cuddly, not thin and aloof like these two; and their pale faces and ginger hair put him off. His wife would not have agreed anyway. They now had a family of their own at last. Two children had arrived in quick succession, a boy and a girl. Marjorie had been very pleased, especially with the boy.

Over the next few years the Habenhowe twins grew up more or less normally—depending on what view was taken of their pranks and escapades. Some villagers spoke as though the girls were juvenile delinquents. Others, more charitable, regarded Georgina and Georgette as no worse than most of the village children. Odder, maybe, but no worse.

At school they upset their teachers by often changing places in class or in games. "Which one are you—Georgina or Georgette?" a harassed teacher would demand. Whatever the answer there was no way of telling whether or not it was the truth because the twins took a delight in confusing everyone. They called each other 'Georgie'. Only rarely, when it suited them, would they use their actual names in speaking to other children and then they short-

ened them: "I'm Gina" or "I'm Getty". Their classmates
treated them as one unit instead of two individuals and
they would address the pair of them when they spoke.
Usually only one twin answered. Georgina and Gorgette
kept to themselves in school and discouraged the friend-
ship of other children. Out of school they confined their
contacts to Hugh Cole and Robert Oakleigh who remained
their only friends.

The first time the twins stole anything it was Mrs
Linnet's milk. The old lady swore it was Georgette. "I see'd
her! I see'd her!" she railed. Mrs Linnet was one of the few
people who claimed to be able to tell one twin from the
other, although no one believed her. Georgette said it was
Georgina who stole the milk and Georgina said it was
Georgette and they exchanged a secret smile—one of them
lying her head off and the other one conniving at it.

They began to make simultaneous raids on the village
shops. While Georgette was plundering the sweetshop,
running from the shop with a fistful of chocolate bars,
Georgina would be helping herself to apples from the
greengrocer's further up the High Street. By the time Ted,
the policeman, arrived at their home to sort things out, the
evidence had vanished. Not that there was much he could
do because, as he told their harassed mother, no one could
tell him with certainty which girl had stolen what. He
recommended chastising both girls which is what Gladys
did. It didn't stop them thieving but it appeased the shopkeepers.

When Georgina and Georgette started stealing money
Gladys appealed to the Reverend Gaye for help. In a sense,
it was his problem because they didn't keep the money—
they posted it in one of the money boxes screwed to the
church wall. It was the one labelled SEAMEN'S
MISSION. Richard Gaye had a technique for dealing with
wrongdoers. He found it particularly effective with
children. He simply gave them the Hellfire and Damnation routine. "God is watching . . . God will punish you . . .
YOU WILL BURN IN HELL."

Unfortunately, this didn't work with the Habenhowe
girls. They wanted to know how he knew what Hell was
like if he'd never been there. The Reverend Gaye

wondered if this was a judgement upon him for having tampered with the authorised version of the Baptismal service when he christened them.

The Tanniford fete, with its stalls and sideshows, attracted people from miles around. The fete was held every year at Mayfield Hall and in the year that Henry Mayfield's son, Justin, won the fancy-dress competition the proceeds were in aid of a new village hall.

Mrs Mayfield had made a tour of the stalls and was delighted to find how well they were doing. It was a perfect summer's day and there was every sign that the takings would be high. She went in search of her husband to tell him the good news. He was standing at the Home-Made Wine stall sampling the products.

"We look like setting a new record for the takings this year," she told him.

"Good, good." Mayfield held up his glass. "It's a great year for the wine too," he said, winking at Wally Kronks who was serving behind the counter. "Why don't you try a glass, Marge?"

She hated being called Marge but she bit back a retort and forced a smile for Wally's benefit. "Not now, thank you. It's time for the fancy-dress parade. I must find the vicar and tell him he's judging."

"I thought *you* were," her husband said.

"I was, but I can't now that Justin has entered, can I?"

"No, I suppose not." Mayfield gazed moodily at the children who were gathering for the parade. His son, Justin, was impossible to miss. He was dressed-up as Shirley Temple in a short frock and wearing a wig of golden ringlets. "He looks a right sissy."

"No he doesn't," his wife replied defensively. "That's an excellent costume and he spent hours practising the part."

"I'll bet he did," Mayfield said contemptuously. His eyebrows contracted. "Who are those two next to him? The ones talking to Robin Hood . . . young Robert Oakleigh, that is. If they're village kids I don't know them."

Mrs Mayfield glanced at the group of children. She sniffed. "I should have thought you'd recognise your goddaughters."

"Georgina and Georgette?" He stared incredulously. "I would never have believed it. Who are they meant to be?"

"Bonnie and Clyde." She saw his blank look. "Bank robbers. *Gangsters*. Apropriate, don't you think?" she said acidly and walked away to find the Reverend Gaye.

Mayfield sighed. That was the trouble with Marjorie. Always exaggerating a person's faults—unless of course it was Justin. Justin could do no wrong in his mother's eyes. She wasn't like that with Estelle, her first born, who seemed forever to be on the receiving end of Marjorie's sharp tongue. He'd been delighted when his wife gave birth to a baby girl eight years ago, after they'd tried for so long to have children. But Estelle had been a disappointment to him. She whined and she was thin and snappy like her mother. As for Justin who was born a year later . . . he was more like a girl than a boy. Mayfield's eyes returned to where his son was preening himself and prancing about among the children assembling for the competition. His lip curled. The boy was even acting like a girl. It made Mayfield uncomfortable just to watch him. He turned his back and picked up another bottle of wine from the stall. He squinted at the label. "Let's try this one, Wally."

Mrs Mayfield tracked down the vicar at one of the souvenir stalls. He was busily selling brass-rubbings taken from the ancient brasses in the floor of the church.

"But I don't know anything about judging fancy-dress, Mrs Mayfield," he protested when she informed him of what she wanted him to do.

"It's quite simple, vicar," she said firmly. "I'll explain it to you on the way to the announcer's tent."

In no time at all a bewildered Reverend Gaye found himself in the centre of a circle of children in fancy-dress. The theme they had been given for this year's competition was: famous people, real or imaginary. The vicar peered around him shortsightedly, confused by the array of costumes. There was Robin Hood, Long John Silver, Maid Marian and . . . Good Heavens! Frankenstein. Billy Staton was frighteningly realistic as the monster. He decided to make a tour of the circle to exchange a few words with each of the competitors. He'd been told to look for ingenuity,

originality and realism in portraying the character. He
approached a girl in a short dress. She did a little dance
and then sang "On the Good Ship, Lollypop."

"Ah, I know who you are, my dear," said the vicar,
"you're Shirley Temple." It struck him that she wasn't
very original and that any girl of the right age could have
done this. The acting was good though. "What's your
name, little girl?"

The girl's voice modulated. "I'm not a girl. I'm Justin . . .
Justin Mayfield."

Astonished, the Reverend Gaye scrutinised the face
below the golden ringlets, only now realising that the hair
was not real but a wig.

"Oh, that's very good, Justin," he murmured, "very good
indeed."

He moved on to Bonnie and Clyde. With some difficulty
he recognised Bonnie as one of the Habenhowe twins. The
Clyde character in the trilby hat and waistcoat who was
pointing a sub machine-gun at him foxed the vicar for a
moment. However, having encountered a boy dressed as a
girl he wasn't to be taken in a second time. This must be
the other twin, he guessed, although it was hard to tell in
those clothes. He eyed the one in the long tight skirt and
the make-up style of the Thirties. "Georgette?" he asked
tentatively.

The face with the heavily-rouged cheeks and carmined
lips stared coldly back at him. "The name's Bonnie and
don't you forget it, buster," she snapped in a mock
American accent.

"And I'm Clyde Barrow," snarled her companion, pointing the sub-machine-gun menacingly at the vicar's
abdomen, "and if you don't stop pestering my dame I'm
gonna blow your guts out all over the greenstuff!"

"Er . . . yes, most impressive," said the vicar.

He completed his inspection and set the competitors
parading round in a circle for the benefit of the spectators
while he considered his decision. Henry Mayfield nearly
choked on his wine when he heard the result announced
over the loudspeakers.

"For originality, ingenuity and realism," boomed the
vicar's voice, "I award first prize to Justin Mayfield for his

portrayal of Shirley Temple."

Mayfield watched in disgust as his son held out the hem of his dress and executed a deep curtsy, giving a full display of his sister's frilly pants in the process. A few moments later when Justin came running up to him excited by his success, Mayfield hid his discomfort in front of Wally Kronks by teasing the boy.

"Give us a kiss then, Shirley Temple," he said with a grin. Justin tried to pull away but his father seized him and, lifting him up, kissed him on the mouth. Justin fought madly. Roaring with laughter Mayfield turned him over in his arms and delivered a resounding smack to his thinly-covered bottom before setting him down again. Fighting back tears of humiliation, Justin ran off. Still laughing, Mayfield watched him go. No doubt he'd be running to his mother to be coddled and fussed over.

Justin did not run to his mother, however. He slipped round to the rear of the house and into a walled garden where he could shed his tears in private. He stood by the edge of an ornamental pond confused and disturbed by his emotions. He was upset by the way his father had treated him but he was remembering another feeling . . . the feeling of his sister's silky undergarments against his skin. The pleasure of seeing himself in the mirror as he slipped the dress over his head. He stared at his reflection in the still water of the pond and willed the thrilling sensation to return.

A shadow fell across the water and Justin saw a second reflection alongside his own. Startled, he looked up. The twisted face of Frankenstein's monster loomed over him.

"Hullo, girlie." Billy Staton smirked at the expression of alarm on Justin's face. He'd seen Justin leave the fete and had followed him partly out of curiosity and partly out of devilment. Billy enjoyed playing a monster and when he saw Justin standing alone by the pond he couldn't resist frightening him. He put a heavy hand on the boy's shoulder. "Know what the monster does when he meets a little girl? He kills her and throws her in the water."

"No he doesn't," Justin said stoutly. "I've seen the film on telly. He just walks off and leaves her."

"Ah, they cut the bad bit out on telly," Billy told him. "In

the actual film the monster picks her up and strangles her.
Then he tosses her body in the lake." He leered horribly
and was rewarded by tremors of fear in Justin's face.

"I'm not afraid of you, Billy Staton," Justin said bravely.
But he was and his lower lip was quivering.

With a throaty chuckle Billy grasped his small victim
round the waist and raised him high above his head. He
had no intention of really throwing the boy into the pond
but Justin didn't know that and he began screaming
hysterically. Billy enjoyed the situation immensely as he
tossed Justin in the air, caught him and dangled him head
down over the water.

"Put him down!" a voice behind them shouted. Billy
turned round still holding his kicking captive and saw
Robert Oakleigh approaching in the garb of Robin Hood.

"Piss off, Oakleigh," he growled. "We're having a bit of
fun."

"Leave him alone. He's only half your age. Pick on
someone your own size," Robert said angrily.

"Like you, you mean?" Billy sniggered, dropping Justin
on the ground like a bundle of rags and squaring up to his
opponent.

Robert raised his fists. Staton was heavier than he was
and a year older. It would be fatal to let him in close.
Summoning up his boxing knowledge he kept his distance
and moved around waiting for an opening. Justin lay on
the ground, watching. Robert felt responsible for him since
they went to the same school and because at the time
Justin started in preparatory school Mrs Mayfield had
asked him to see that he wasn't bullied. When he saw Billy
Staton sneaking after the boy, Robert had followed to see
what he was up to.

Staton made a clumsy lunge at him and Robert side-
stepped and punched him hard on the side of the head.
Staton swore violently and lunged again. This time Robert
delivered a powerful uppercut to his jaw. Staton's head
snapped back and he only just managed to stay on his feet.
He shook his head groggily and stood back.

"I'm not fighting over that little nancy-boy," he sneered.
He walked away and then at a safe distance he called out:
"You're both nancy-boys! And you go to a school for nancy-

boys!"

Justin came to his feet and smoothed down his dress. "Thanks, Oakleigh. I think he really meant to throw me in."

"That's all right, Mayfield," Robert said. "Come on, I expect your mother will be wondering where you are."

At the Home-Made Wine stall Henry Mayfield replenished his glass and stared morosely at the Habenhowe girls and Hugh Cole in the distance. Wherever the twins were, Hughie was never far away. One reason Mayfield was more kindly disposed to the twins than most people was that they were good to Hughie. The lad was seventeen now and as backward as ever. Four years at an ESN school had made no difference. He would never be able to make his own way in the world. Mayfield wished he knew of something he could do to make things better for Hughie.

In the background a big drum began beating. A moment later there was a fanfare of trumpets.

SEVEN

Twenty high-stepping drum majorettes in scarlet dresses, long white gloves and white ankle-boots came marching into the grounds of the fete. They ranged between eight and twelve years of age and on their heads they wore toy-soldier hats covered with gold braid. The brass band accompanying them peeled off to one side and halted and the girls began an exhibition of marching and counter-marching.

Henry Mayfield, now slightly drunk, moved forward for a better view of the colourful spectacle. As the files advanced and retreated his attention focused on one particular girl. This little charmer was about nine, he thought. She seemed wonderfully alive and full of joy as she made an energetic about-turn which sent her dress swirling and caused the short cape to fly out from her shoulders. She was the leading girl on the outside file and each time she marched towards him he deliberately tried to catch her eye. After several attempts he succeeded and he gave her a wide smile. To his delight she held his eyes and smiled back. From then on, every time she reached the end of her forward march they exchanged smiles before she turned away again.

Ruth Staton was faithfully following the instructions that had been dinned into her at every training session. "Look happy! Show your teeth. Legs up, up, up and *smile*." Ruth did as she'd been taught. She high-stepped for all she was worth to make her flared skirt bounce up and down and when a jolly-looking man with brown, curly hair kept grinning at her she gave him dazzling smiles in return.

The display ended and Mayfield clapped enthusiastically and returned to Wally Kronks's stall. The troop of majorettes broke up and the girl he'd been watching and another girl—Dolly Kronks—ran in his direction. As they approached, Mayfield realised that he knew the little charmer who had captivated him. She was Molly Staton's daughter, Ruth.

"Got any orange, dad?" Dolly gasped, clutching the edge of the counter. "We're hot and we're dry."

Close to, Mayfield saw that she was made up with eye-black and lipstick. He glanced slyly sideways at Ruth. She was made up too. Wisps of ash-blonde hair strayed below her hat. Her lips were parted and her upper lip was moist with perspiration. As she breathed heavily in and out, her chest strained against the satin bodice of her dress.

"There's no orange here love, no soft drinks of any kind, I'm afraid," Wally said.

"Oh . . . *dad* . . ." Dolly wailed.

"There's orange squash in the house." Mayfield spoke quickly and impulsively, his eyes on Ruth. She tilted her head back and looked up at him with wide blue eyes.

Wally began: "Now, Mr Mayfield, there's no need for you—"

"It's no trouble," Mayfield insisted, "and I'm sure these girls deserve a nice cold drink after all that marching." He smiled at them. "I'll take you up there." He shepherded them away before Wally could suggest that they went across to the drinks stall on the other side of the field. He was heady with wine and felt reckless. He'd find an excuse to send Dolly Kronks back quickly so that he could be alone with Ruth. He longed to touch her and take hold of her.

An hour later, as the fete was ending, Billy Staton looked for his sister to take her home. He hadn't seen her since she'd been prancing up and down with the major-ettes. He spotted her friend Dolly Kronks.

"Where's Ruthie?"

"Up the house with old man Mayfield."

"What's she doing there?"

"I dunno. He's showing her round or something."

Billy strolled to the house and then round to the rear. He passed an open kitchen window and a woman washing up at the sink called out:

"Hullo Frankenstein, what do you want?"

"I'm looking for me sister—I think she's with Mr Mayfield."

"They're at the top of the field in the stables." Billy nodded and sauntered on.

In the stable-yard Henry Mayfield stood beside a pony steadying it. He bent down and lifted Ruth up and on to the pony's back. She clung to him nervously:

"I'm frightened," she said. "I don't really like horses."

"There's nothing to be afraid of," he told her soothingly. "You're quite safe." He put an arm round her waist and held her.

Earlier he'd shown her the fishpond and Estelle's rabbits and they'd wandered through a wood to the stables. When, now and again, he risked a trembling caress, Ruth responded eagerly as though hungry for affection. Mayfield was enchanted by her.

He lifted the reins over the horse's head and showed Ruth how to hold them. Then he adjusted the stirrups and guided her booted feet into them. "There you are." He stepped back.

Confident now, she looked down at him, regal in her majorette's uniform and tall hat. "Walk me around," she demanded imperiously.

He laughed and gave a mock bow. "Yes, your majesty." He led the pony round the stable-yard by its bridle.

"It feels ever so hard," Ruth said after a while, wriggling about in the saddle.

"Well, that's hardly the right outfit for riding. You should be wearing jodhpurs or jeans."

"I need to go to the bathroom," she said gravely.

"What? Oh—er . . ." He halted the pony. "Over there— the door in the corner." He reached up to help her down. As he lifted her from the saddle her arms went round his neck. "I wish you were my daddy," she breathed in his ear. "So do I," he murmured impetuously. He kissed her cheek and held her tightly.

That was how Billy Staton found them as he rounded the entrance to the yard. He stopped short, puzzled by the sight. Henry Mayfield saw him and hastily lowered Ruth to the ground.

"Just showing Ruth the ponies," he explained as she ran to the toilet in the corner of the yard.

"Ruth don't like horses," Billy said.

"I know. I've been teaching her not to be afraid of them."

"Oh yeh," said Billy, indifferently.

"Do you like horses?"

"Oh yeh," Billy said again. "Don't get no chance to ride

though."

Mayfield regarded him thoughtfully. "Would you like to come up here and ride?"

"Oh yeh," said Billy for the third time, wondering what the catch would be. Have to muck out the stables for a week, he supposed.

"Very well. You . . . and your sister . . . come along next Saturday afternoon." The slight emphasis on 'and your sister' was not lost on Billy. No Ruth, no riding.

There was the sound of a cistern flushing and Ruth reappeared. "We'll be here," Billy promised.

"Hadn't you better ask your mother first?"

"She won't mind," Billy said confidently. The fact was that Molly Staton had very little control over her son these days. If Billy wanted to take his sister to Mayfield Hall to go riding, then he would.

That had been the start of the visits to Mayfield Hall. They had quickly become regular events. At first Billy and Ruth, Mayfield and his daughter, Estelle, had all gone riding together. Soon, however, Billy found himself sent off on two-hour rides with Estelle while Mayfield and Ruth stayed behind. Billy didn't mind. Estelle was competent on a horse and the riding was better without Ruth tagging along. They usually returned to the house at about four o'clock and soon after there would be a sumptuous tea when Mrs Mayfield came in. Saturday was her day at the Women's Institute.

One afternoon when they were out together Estelle told him: "I don't like your sister. She's always making up to my dad."

On his return Billy asked Ruth: "What d'you do all the time we're out?"

She was evasive. "Play with Justin . . . talk to Mr Mayfield . . . things like that."

Then some months later there had been a bad thunderstorm when Billy was riding with Estelle. She'd moaned that she was frightened and they'd returned to the house an hour early. Estelle went to her room to change and Billy went to look for Ruth. In the playroom he found Justin kneeling on the floor talking to his pet hamster in its cage.

"Where's Ruthie?"

Justin shrugged. "Around."

Billy put out a hand and ran his fingers through Justin's dark curls. He tightened his grip and forced Justin's head back. The soft brown eyes gazd up at him. There was a brightness in them but no fear.

"She's in the study with dad. He said he doesn't want to be disturbed."

Billy had gone to the study door and listened. He could hear nothing, no sound of voices. He pushed open the heavy door and heard the sound of flurried movements inside. When he had the door fully open and looked round it Mayfield was sitting in a deep armchair and Ruth was standing by the bookshelves with an open book in her hand. The room felt close and there was an atmosphere . . . nothing Billy could put his finger on . . . something he sensed.

"You'd been sitting on his lap," he accused later as they walked home down the hill into Tanniford.

"So? What if I had?"

Billy didn't answer. He hadn't been bothered anyway, only curious. Ruth was ten at the time.

Occasionally, if Estelle was in a sulk or not feeling well, Billy was allowed to go riding on his own. Once, when he was alone and riding along the edge of Tanniford woods he felt an urge to relieve himself. He reined in his horse, dismounted and tethered it to a small tree. He walked a few yards along a narrow footpath into the woods and was about to unfasten his trousers when he became aware of someone further along the path sitting on the ground with his back against a tree. It was Hugh Cole. A cigarette dangled from his mouth.

Billy walked up to him. "Hullo Lofty, what are you doing here?"

Languidly, Hugh removed the cigarette. "Smokin'."

"Smoking's bad for you—stops you growing."

Hugh uttered a hoot of laughter. "I've growed too much already, mum says."

"You'll be taking up drinking next."

"Nah, they won't let me have it in the pub," said Hugh. There was a tacit understanding in the Spreadeagle, the Anchor and the Black Dog that it wouldn't be right to serve Hugh Cole with alcohol, him being so simple.

A sudden idea came into Billy's tortuous mind. He looked around. There was no sign of anyone. "Tell you what, Lofty," he said, "there's a couple of beers back there in me horse's saddlebag. You can try one if you like—see if you like the taste."

"Yeh, O.K. Thanks."

Billy doubled back out of sight. He unslung his shoulder haversack and took out two cartons of lemonade which he carried with him when he was riding in case he became thirsty. He opened one and poured the contents on the ground.

Some moments later he rejoined Hugh Cole. "Here y'are." He held out one of the cartons. Hugh took it and squinted at the label.

"It says 'Beer'," Billy said, "same as mine. Look." He showed him the other carton.

Hugh couldn't read but he could see that the shapes of the words were the same. "Smells funny," he said.

"That's 'cos you're not used to the smell of beer." Billy took a large mouthful from his own container. "Let's see you drink it down like they do on the films," he said. "Put your head back and swallow it fast."

Hugh nodded and raised the carton to his mouth.

"Don't Hughie!" Suddenly the Habenhowe twins materialised from the undergrowth.

Billy froze, uncertain what to do. The two girls advanced. One of them took the carton of amber fluid from Hugh, held it to her nose and sniffed. Her mouth wrinkled in distaste. Billy dropped his carton of lemonade and turned to run. He heard a snapped word of command and before he'd taken three steps Hugh's arms fastened round him in an iron band. Another command and he was forced to his knees, with Hugh squatting behind him pinioning his arms to his sides.

He looked up into two cold, hard faces. One girl held Hugh's carton to his mouth. "*You* drink it."

"It was only a joke," he said.

"Drink."

"It's piss!" he said desperately.

"No it isn't, it's beer," she said mockingly. "You said so

yourself. Drink it."

He realised then what they intended. He began to struggle frantically but it was useless. Big as Billy was, Hugh was bigger and stronger.

"*Drink!*"

He clamped his mouth shut and shook his head. The other girl moved to the side of him and gripped his head, holding it still. The girl with the carton pinched his nostrils between thumb and forefinger. When he opened his mouth for air she tipped in the liquid, released his nose and held his mouth closed until he swallowed. They weren't satisfied until he'd taken two more mouthfuls of urine. Then they released him and stood staring impassively as he lay on the ground gagging and retching.

"You ever try tricks on Hughie again," said one girl.

"And we'll put a spell on you," said the other. They went on speaking alternately like a double-act.

"We'll make a wax model of you and stick pins in it."

"You'll have terrible pains in your belly."

"And if we don't take the pins out you'll *die*."

By the time he finished spewing they had vanished along with Hughie.

There was murder in Billy Staton's heart as he rode back to Mayfield Hall. One day, he promised himself, one day he'd make them pay. He'd have his revenge.

EIGHT

Gladys Habenhowe's drinking had begun soon after her husband drowned. It wasn't that she was depressed by his death or even particularly upset by it. The simple fact was that she became better off because of the insurance money and could afford to indulge herself with a bottle of whisky whenever she felt like it. And she felt like it more and more as the years passed and her problems with Georgina and Georgette continued. They were thirteen now and she had to accept that her relationship with them had ceased to be that of mother and daughters. However hard she tried to gain their confidence, she failed. They kept her out. She was an outsider. A friend perhaps—yes, she liked to think of herself as their friend—but she was no more than that. There was a kinship between Georgina and Georgette that Gladys was unable to share.

The rift between Gladys and her daughters dated back some time. She'd tried to be a good mother to them, God knows she had, Gladys told herself. It had been the tricks they'd plagued her with that she couldn't stand. Forever pretending to be each other . . . mixing up their belongings . . . refusing to answer to their names. What Gladys had once looked upon as intriguing and lovable—their sameness, the impossibility of telling them apart—suddenly became a frustration and an aggravation. She didn't mind them confusing other people but she could not abide them deceiving *her*, their own mother. In Gladys's book it was wicked to deceive your mother and she'd set out to put a stop to it. That had been her undoing.

The battle of wills had gone on for weeks as Gladys tried to bring an end to Georgina and Georgette's constant fooling of her as to which of them was which. She'd punished them harder and harder, frightening herself with her violence. The more she punished them the more obstinate and withdrawn they became. She'd had the terrible feeling that it was like whipping cream: the longer and harder you whipped, the stiffer and thicker it became. In the end she'd had to admit defeat. It had been a turning point. From then on their attitude to her had been different; and she had forced them closer to each other and further away from her.

Now, Gladys no longer tried to make them identify themselves when they didn't want to, so there were no arguments on that score. They were obedient about most other things. They helped around the house. They were polite and, despite what the village said, they didn't make trouble. At least . . . Gladys shrugged and reached for the whisky bottle. She never knew what they were up to these days.

Sometimes when, like this evening, she was alone in the house, she would pour herself half a glass of neat spirit and sit slowly sipping it and thinking. A glass of whisky soothed her. "Only one glass," she murmured, "to last me till they come in." She worried when they were out after dark. It wasn't sensible for thirteen-year-olds to be out late at night. Not outside the village anyway and she was pretty sure they wandered further afield than Tanniford. It was no use asking them where they went though. They wouldn't have told her. Probably they were out with Robert. She was glad they were still friends with Dr Oakleigh's son. A nice boy he was turning out to be. Of course, Hughie would be with them too so they'd be quite safe. Hughie would see no harm came to them.

The whisky began to take effect and she started nodding, half asleep in her armchair. Dear, stupid Hughie, bless him. Carol hadn't deserved that tragedy. Such an innocent young thing she'd been when Mayfield latched on to her. He'd had his fun there all right. Her parents should have stood by her, poor little bitch. Still, I was as good as a mother to her, Gladys told herself. And all the time Henry Mayfield practically on his knees to me, begging for help. Got her some pills, didn't I? And when they didn't work didn't I fix her up with a place to have the baby and no questions asked? Should have had the boy adopted. I could have arranged it. But Carol wanted to keep him. Silly kid gave herself to Lionel Cole in return for a home for her and the baby. *He'd* had the best of *that* bargain. Dribbling at the mouth he'd been over having Carol for a bride. Gladys sighed. Poor Carol. Poor me. Neither of us had much luck with our men . . . or our children. She began snoring peacefully.

"It's not working tonight," said Georgette. They were in a hideaway they'd made in a small archway under a railway embankment. The embankment carried a single-track railway that joined the Tanniford line south of the village. The track had been abandoned years ago. It had been built to connect the small fishing port at the mouth of the river with the railway at Tanniford but before it opened the fishing industry there had declined. The line had no longer been needed and it was left unfinished.

"That's because Robert's here," said Georgina. "He's putting Hughie off."

"O.K., I'll go outside," Robert said. "But *I* think the trouble is that he's cold." He pushed aside the sacking across the entrance and stepped outside. Beyond the frost-covered fields he could see the lights of Tanniford in the distance. He shivered and pulled his anorak closer about him. He doubted if the twins could do what they'd said they could even if it hadn't been so cold.

"We can put Hughie into a trance," they'd said. "Would you like to see?"

"Yes, all right." Robert had been sceptical, but curious. Also he was flattered that the twins were actually offering to share a secret with him because they hardly ever volunteered information about themselves. Although he knew things about them that other people didn't, they were things he'd learned either by accident or by observation, not because they'd told him. The occasional glimpses he had of their private selves imposed on Robert a strong sense of loyalty to Georgina and Georgette and he wouldn't talk about them to anyone—not even his father. They knew this and that was why they trusted him and remained friends with him.

"Have you ever noticed the pattern of their hair whorls?" his father asked once.

"No, I haven't," Robert answered diffidently. He had, in fact.

"Well, look boy, look! They're identical. They run counter-clockwise and—"

"My dear," said Mrs Oakleigh, interrupting her

husband, "must you be so clinical about the girls' hair?"

"The boy intends to be a doctor, doesn't he? He stould observe these things. The Habenhowe twins are a unique opportunity."

"Georgina and Georgette aren't specimens to be observed," Robert told his father angrily. "They're *girls*. They're my friends."

Inside the hideout behind Robert, Georgette wrapped sacking and newspapers around Hugh. He was lying on the frame of an old iron bedstead. It was one of the pieces of furniture he had helped the twins to drag there from the dump beside the shipyard. Two candles in bottles on a box by the bed provided illumination. Georgina bent over Hugh and began her rigmarole for the second time.

"You're warm, Hughie, warm and comfortable. Listen to my voice . . . listen . . . your eyes are beginning to feel heavy . . . very heavy . . ." She extended her index finger and placed the tip in the centre of his forehead just below the hairline. "Close your eyes. Now look up . . . look up inside your head to where you can feel my finger." Obediently Hugh's eyeballs rolled upwards behind his eyelids. Georgina's voice continued in a flat monotone.

A while later Georgette drew aside the sacking at the entrance. "You can come in now," she told Robert.

He stepped inside. Hugh Cole lay motionless on the bedframe with his eyes closed.

"You can talk to him," Georgina said. "He won't answer because he only responds to my voice. And he can't open his eyes."

Robert knelt beside Hugh. Experimentally, he pulled down the bottom lid of one of Hugh's eyes. He could see only white and he quickly released the eyelid again. Gingerly, he prised open the top lid with his thumb. The eyeball was turned up into the head and only part of the iris was showing. He took out a penlight torch he'd brought with him and shone it directly into the pupil. There was no contraction—not even a flicker. Robert went to the foot of the bed and removed one of Hugh's shoes. He tickled the sole of his foot. There was no reaction. He turned to the twins. "How do you do it?" he asked in awe.

"We read it up in a book," one of them said, "and then we

practised on each other until we could do it."

"You mean you can hypnotise each other too?"

"Oh, *that's* easy. Would you like to see?"

He nodded. One girl sat down on the bedframe beside the reclining Hugh. The other one stood over her and, placing a hand on her sister's head, leaned down and murmured in her ear. The girl on the bed immediately shut her eyes and flopped back in a prone position.

"She's only pretending," Robert said.

"She's not. She's in a trance." The tone was slightly sharp and he was certain that it was Georgina who had done the hypnotising—if indeed that's what it was. Georgette was imperceptibly softer, a shade warmer towards him. The difference seemed only to apply to him because other people could not detect it. They said there was nothing to choose between the twins . . . they were a pair of cold-hearted freaks.

"I'll show you whether she's pretending or not." Georgina pulled a pin from the lapel of her coat and, bending over Georgette, she said in a matter-of-fact voice: "Your left hand feels frozen. You have no feeling in it . . . no feeling at all." She looked up at Robert. "Take her left hand and hold it up."

He lifted the limp hand by the wrist and fingers. Although he was half prepared for what happened next he winced as Georgina pushed the pin firmly into her sister's upturned palm until it was deeply embedded in the flesh. She pulled the pin out again. "Satisfied?" Georgina's eyes gleamed brightly at Robert.

He swallowed and nodded. He lowered Georgette's hand gently and sat down on one of the packing cases that did duty as a seat. "You managed to induce a trance very quickly," he commented.

"We've conditioned ourselves to respond to a single code word. We've tried to do the same with Hughie but he's not very good at it. It takes a long time to put him under."

"Hadn't you better wake them up now?" Robert asked uneasily.

"It's no problem," Georgina said confidently. She leaned down and spoke quietly to her sister. A few seconds later Georgette sighed and sat up. Georgina moved to the other side of the bed and bent over Hugh Cole.

"I'm going to start counting, Hughie, and as I do you'll begin to wake up. When I reach five and clap my hands you'll be completely awake. One . . . two . . . three . . . four . . . five." She clapped her hands. Hugh didn't stir. She tried again, counting and clapping once more. Hugh remained still.

Robert became alarmed. Suppose they couldn't wake Hugh from his trance? Suppose his father had to be called out to attend to him? He was good-tempered about most things but he would be furious about something like this. There would be the devil of a row.

"What are you going to do?"

"Oh, don't worry," Georgina said airily. "He does this sometimes. He'll fall into an ordinary sleep and wake up when he's ready. There's no need to fuss. We just have to sit and wait."

They sat in silence. Being silent for long periods was something Robert was accustomed to with the Habenhowe twins. However long they went without speaking though, Georgina and Georgette would be totally aware of each other's thoughts and feelings. It was uncanny. As uncanny as the time he'd been fooling around with Georgette one day in their home in North Street. Georgina had been in another room. Teasingly, Robert had suddenly tickled Georgette. Immediately there came a burst of giggling from Georgina in the next room.

"Your sister's laughing," he said in astonishment.

"Well, of course," said Georgette, "you're tickling." She'd been doubled up, her face open and smiling until she saw his surprise and read the question in his eyes. At once her expression had become guarded and she'd added quickly: "She heard me giggling. We always set each other off." Her expression warned him not to pursue the matter. He was to recall the incident years later when a similar one ocrurred, although in a much more intimate situation. That was when he became convinced that if the feeling experienced by one twin—whether of pain or of pleasure— was intense and acute enough, then in some extraordinary way the other twin felt it also.

Time passed in the hideout under the railway embankment and still Hugh Cole did not wake up.

"Shouldn't you give him a shake and try to bring him out of it?" Robert asked. The twins shook their heads. He took out a packet of cigarettes. He'd started smoking in secret a month ago on his fifteenth birthday. "Cigarette?" Casually he offered the packet to the girls. They shook their heads and watched, wide-eyed, as he made an elaborate ritual of taking out a cigarette, putting it in his mouth and lighting it. He'd recently learned to inhale and he drew in a lungful of smoke and blew it out through his nostrils, enjoying the impression he was making on Georgina and Georgette.

Behind him Hugh Cole stirred and sat up. "Wass goin' on?" he mumbled. "Someone smokin'?"

Billy Staton's afternoon ride had been spoiled by heavy rain and by Estelle constantly criticising the way he handled his horse. It didn't improve his temper to find Ruth more than usually cheerful and happy as they walked home from Mayfield Hall.

"What you so chuffed about then?" Billy asked sourly.

"Nothing," she said defensively.

"There's *something*," he insisted. "Come on, what is it? What you bin up to?"

Ruth put her head in the air and marched onward. "I'll tell mum you've been letting old Mayfield mess about with you," Billy threatened.

Ruth stopped abruptly. "You have to make everything dirty, don't you?" she said fiercely. "Mr Mayfield is nice . . . very nice. He's kind and he likes me. He likes me a *lot*, so there!" She stamped her foot in anger. "And you keep your big nose out of things or I'll tell mum what *you* used to do to me!"

Billy went pale. He hadn't thought she would remember that far back. Triumphantly, Ruth walked on. It wasn't often she managed to best her brother and she enjoyed her victory. What if she did kiss and cuddle with Mr Mayfield? It was no more that she'd have done with her dad—well, a little more, perhaps—if her dad loved her, which he didn't, and if she had a dad, which she didn't, leastways not really because he never came home now, or wrote, or sent her presents.

Mr Mayfield had given her a lovely present this afternoon. A real gold cross on a gold chain. It was for her twelfth birthday which wasn't yet, but not far off. She wasn't to show it to anyone till then, nor to let on that it was twenty-two-carat gold. "That'll be *our* secret," he'd said. No one would know because you had to look at some funny squiggly marks with a magnifying glass to find out. It was very, *very* valuable and she would treasure it all her life. Mr Mayfield had told her she was very pretty as he'd fastened the chain round her neck and she'd been extra specially nice to him afterwards.

In his study Henry Mayfield sat chewing his lip after Ruth had left. This madness had to stop. He was playing with dynamite. He adopted all kinds of subterfuges to be alone with Ruth . . . taking her for walks, developing photographs in the darkroom with her, showing her the hayloft in the stables and so on. Yet it amazed him that his wife didn't suspect anything. He imagined his guilt to be written all over his face. But all Marjorie had ever said was: "You're always very jolly after the Station children have been here." Perhaps she did suspect and didn't care. She almost seemed to make a point of being out of the house when they came.

In the beginning he'd thought his attachment to such a young girl was a result of the onset of middle-age—a yearning for his lost youth. He'd expected to become bored with her and to find the bizarre infatuation wearing off. Instead it had grown more intense. Ruth had been pathetically eager for attention and admiration—both of which he readily lavished upon her. It had been a fatal combination . . . her needs exactly matching his own hunger.

He'd meant this afternoon's present to be a parting gift—an end to the relationship—as well as a birthday present. When it had come to the point though, he couldn't bring himself to make the break. His need of her warmth and undemanding physical affection was relentless. It was far stronger than his common sense or his conscience.

Henry Mayfield buried his head in his hands and groaned like a man in pain.

NINE

Georgina and Georgette achieved puberty in slow stages. The process was unhurried and took a long time to complete. They entered this new phase of their lives as rather plain, freckle-faced girls with gawky figures and bright ginger hair—though woe betide anyone foolish enough to shout "Ginger!" at them. The girls were quick and they were fierce. Many a boy discovered to his cost that they attacked like a pair of tigresses and that it was far worse than being set upon by another boy.

The village children had grown wary of the two thirteen-year-olds. None of them, except Hugh Cole and Robert Oakleigh, sought their company. The Habenhowe twins with their pale faces and pale-blue eyes were to be avoided. As like as not, people said, they would make a waxen image of you and stick pins in it and then you'd be ill. Or else they would fix you with one of their unwinking stares and put the "fluence" on you so you didn't know what you were doing.

There was a deal of superstition in Tanniford and some inhabitants with long memories maintained that Harry Habenhowe had been lost at sea because at the launching of the *Alacrity* his daughters had cast a spell over the ship. It had caused the vessel to come sideways off her launching ways. The twins were standing on that side . . . alone . . . *willing it to happen*. No one had offered a really satisfactory explanation of the disaster. It didn't help for others, like Dr Oakleigh and the Reverend Gaye, to point out that Georgina and Georgette had never harmed anyone who hadn't harmed them in some way first. That's *why* the twins put the "fluence" on the *Alacrity*, argued the superstitious ones. Hadn't the ship nearly crushed them to death? And everyone knew their father hadn't liked them and they'd done well out of his death.

The changes in Georgina and Georgette occurred gradually over the two years between thirteen and fifteen. The ginger hair darkened to an attractive chestnut colour. The eyes darkened too, into a shade of violet, or perhaps they had been that shade all along and the hair-colouring had spoiled it. The freckles vanished and their figures became decidedly shapely. Georgina and Georgette changed from pale, plain-looking girls into bubbling, eye-flashing beauties; and, like butterflies emerging from their chrysalids, they spread their wings and caught everyone's eye. The villagers wagged their heads knowingly and muttered that there'd be a new kind of trouble in the village now.

The first signs of alarm came from the school. The Headmaster called to see Gladys.

"As you know, Mrs Habenhowe, we're not a uniformed school and the girls and boys are allowed to dress as they please." He smiled at her. "Within reason, that is," he added firmly.

Gladys nodded and hoped the Headmaster would not stay long. She was dying for a drink. She deliberated the wisdom of offering the Head a whisky rather than tea or coffee. If he refused she couldn't very well have one herself. Still, she'd be no worse off than at present.

"Will you have a drink, Headmaster? Whisky?" She tried to make it sound as though tea and coffee weren't available, which they weren't so far as Gladys was concerned. Since the twins had blossomed out she had abandoned any pretence of being responsible for them and had taken to the bottle openly and with relief. "I've brought them this far," she told herself, not altogether truthfully. "They're on their own now."

The Headmaster cleared his throat. "A whisky would be very welcome, thank you, Mrs Habenhowe."

The Head's eyebrows rose as Gladys downed the neat spirit in one swallow. She felt better with a stiff drink inside her and her face relaxed into a smile.

"What have my girls been up to then?"

The Head took a cautious sip of his whisky which he had heavily diluted with water. "Their behaviour has become very . . . well—er . . . provocative lately." He paused and raised his eyes to the ceiling, communing with himself. "Yes. Yes, I think that would be a fair description. Provocative." He lowered his eyes again. "To the boys, I mean," he added hastily, in case she thought he meant the staff.

"Oh yes," said Gladys, who understood full well what he meant.

"But it's really about the way they dress for school that I've come to see you. I'm sure we shall straighten this out quite easily, Mrs Habenhowe," he said, gaining confidence, "but they *have* been spoken to several times and they don't take any notice. That's why I thought I would come and have a word with you myself."

"What's wrong with the way they dress?" Gladys asked, knowing the answer perfectly well and boldly pouring herself a second drink.

The Headmaster watched her in amazement, wondering how much more she would pour into the glass. Gladys didn't stop until it was full. His lips set in a thin line. So, that was the way things were, was it? Gladys held the bottle towards him. He covered his glass with his hand and shook his head.

"I'm afraid we cannot permit high heels—certainly not ones as high as your daughters are wearing," he said stiffly. "And—er plunge necklines really will not do in the classroom, you know."

Gladys took a leisurely mouthful of her drink. Georgina and Georgette had become clothes-conscious all of a sudden. Clothes-mad was probably a more apt description. She had tried to reason with them but they wouldn't listen. Gladys, now fifty-five, wanted a quiet life and she hadn't the stamina to stand up to young teenagers.

"I don't have any say in what my daughters wear," she said. "They have their own money and they don't heed anything I say. *I* can't tell them what to do."

"Do you mean they are beyond parental control?" It was one of the Head's pet phrases—one he had picked up during his attendances at juvenile courts. He found it useful for prodding parents into taking more responsibility for their children. Not so with Gladys Habenhowe however.

She nodded. "Yes," she agreed meekly. "I think you could say that." It brought her relief to admit the fact out loud to someone.

The Headmaster gazed into his whisky, temporarily at a loss. It was not the answer he usually received. He brought out his next ploy. This one invariably worked.

"Well, if *you* won't discipline them, Mrs Habenhowe, then *I* shall have to do it." As a rule parents came quickly to heel when he suggested that. They seldom surrendered the punishment of their children to anyone else. Again Gladys let him down though.

"Yes. Yes, all right."

He'd banked on a protest followed by a promise that she would correct the girls herself. Now that she had virtually granted permission for him to deal with them he didn't know how to use it. Ban them from classes? That would reflect on the school and on him and Heaven knows what drivel the local paper would print about it. He knew what he would have liked to do with the Habenhowe girls but that wasn't even allowed with boys these days. There was a lot to be said for the old days when girls could be caned as well as boys—*and* on the natural place for it.

"I shall speak to them," he promised grimly.

"Would you like to see them now? They're upstairs."

"No," he said hastily. "No, thank you." Much better in his Head's study surrounded by the full weight of his authority.

By next morning he had second thoughts. The girls hadn't been unruly or violent. This was a question of unladylike behaviour, a matter for a woman to handle. He passed the problem to the deputy headmistress.

"Explain to them that they are attracting undesirable interest to themselves," he counselled. "I'm sure they'll understand."

"I imagine that's exactly the sort of interest they want to attract," she retorted waspishly, not at all pleased at being handed the impossible task of curbing the Habenhowe twins.

"Oh, well, handle it anyway you please," the Head said despairingly.

It was out of school, however—in the village—where Georgina and Georgette's flamboyant pubescence caused the biggest ructions. Wolf-whistles, open-eyed admiration from the boys and sideways glances from their fathers made the twins fully aware of the effect they were having upon the male population of Tanniford. Every male for miles around seemed to be competing for their favours and doors that once had been closed to them now stood open.

The girls exploited this new power with verve and enthusiasm and it was not long before the stories began to circulate. A few of the tales were put about by women in the village who had long resented the Habenhowe girls and their strange ways. Resentment turned to malice as their menfolk began chasing after them—"like dogs running after bitches on heat," one woman said vulgarly. Others, more polite, said the twins had become "boy-crazy". Some of the stories came from the lads themselves. It had become every boy's ambition to date the Habenhowe twins and it was only natural for a boy to boast of his success when he did and to render a colourful and exaggerated account of what took place.

One thing was certainly true. You couldn't date just one twin. You had to date the two together and that proved expensive. "But Jesus! It's worth it!" reported one lad ecstatically.

"It's weird man, real weird," said another, "being out with two luscious birds that look exactly the same."

"They do everything together," announced a third, goggle-eyed. "*Everything*!"

The general opinion among the village Romeos was that you hadn't lived until you'd had a night out with the Habenhowe twins.

Robert Oakleigh refused to join in the general scramble for dates with Georgina and Georgette. His pride wouldn't let him. He realised he had no monopoly of the twins simply because he'd known them for so long, but nonetheless he felt they owed him a certain loyalty. The weeks passed however and he saw less and less of them. There were no more evening walks beside the river, no cosy get-togethers in the candle-lit hideout under the railway embankment. He was sad about that and sorely missed their company. When he passed them in the street they seemed like strangers with their startling make-up, elaborate hair-do and smart clothes.

Eventually he swallowed his pride and called at their house to ask if he could take them to the next disco at the village hall. One of them opened a desk diary.

"Let's see . . . that's on Wednesday week . . . oh, sorry." She made a face. "We already have a date for that night." Her finger moved a long way down the page to a blank space. "We're not booked so far for the following week."

"No thanks," he said gruffly. "I have an engagement for that night." It was untrue but he was damned if he'd be fitted into their calendar like every other Tom, Dick and Harry.

"Shall we put you down for our next free evening then?"

"It's all right, thank you," he said woodenly. "I'm rather busy with my studies right now. I'll leave it."

"Suit yourself." Two pairs of eyes regarded him coolly. "Other boys manage to find the time."

He was angry at being bracketed with other boys. Who did they think they were, acting like prima donnas? Plainly they wanted to add him to their list of conquests along with all the village Romeos. Well, he wasn't having that. He walked out in a huff.

The stories about the twins' goings-on grew wilder and more absurd. Robert didn't believe half of them, but he wondered about the others. He was seventeen and full of shining ideals. He would have liked none of the tales to be true.

"You don't see much of Georgina and Georgette these days," his father observed. "Aren't you friends with them any more?"

"Oh yes, I see them occasionally," he answered lightly. "But I don't have much spare time at present with exams coming up next term."

Dr Oakleigh regarded his son doubtfully. He was relieved that Robert was concentrating on his studies unhindered by romantic distractions but on the other hand he didn't care for the unhappy look he'd seen on his face of late. Dr Oakleigh was well aware of the scandalous accounts of Georgina and Georgette's behaviour. Ridiculous gossip about them being alcoholics like their mother. That one of them had an abortion and the other a miscarriage. All this without the knowledge of himself, the local doctor, of course. And the girls not yet sixteen. It was too bad. Dr Oakleigh would have dearly liked to amputate the wagging tongues of the old crones who spread these scurrilous rumours. He laid a sympathetic hand on Robert's shoulder.

"I shouldn't believe all you hear about them" he said.

"I don't," Robert replied quietly.

Hugh Cole also saw less of the twins but that was because he didn't tag along with them when they went out on their dates—which was most of the time. His attachment to Georgina and Georgette, and theirs to him, was as strong as ever. However, Hugh too was developing a new interest.

Unlike the twins, Ruth Staton—a year younger than them—rocketed to puberty very suddenly and very fast. Possibly those continual emotion-stirring sessions with Henry Mayfield had a hothouse effect, bringing her into flower very rapidly. Everything happened in a few short months. She started her periods—her waist went in—her bust came out—and she shot upwards some two or three inches.

Her attitude to Henry Mayfield changed. She remained affectionate but the barricades went up. She permitted no more fondling and petting, no more caressing. And kissing was strictly limited to saying hullo and goodbye. He was sad, yet relieved. Soon she would stop coming altoghether, he realised. The problem had been solved for him. Her brother's visits would also stop and that was a good thing. Mayfield was disturbed by the attachment his son Justin seemed to be forming for Billy Staton.

The end came one day when he tried to negotiate an extra kiss and Ruth said firmly: "No. My boyfriend wouldn't like it."

He forced himself to laugh good-humouredly. "Aha! I have a rival, do I? Who is the dashing swain?"

Her reply staggered him. "Hugh Cole."

He gaped at her, unable to believe she was serious. "But . . ." He searched for suitable words. She saved him the effort.

"I know everyone says Hughie's simple—that he's not all there. But he's not as daft as some people think. And he's ever so kind." She put her head on one side and looked at him with her frank blue eyes. "He's a bit like you, in a way."

He felt as though he'd been kicked in the stomach. *His own son.* The irony of it.

"I shan't be coming again," she said.

"No, I understand." He longed to hold her hard against him for one last time but was afraid of making himself ridiculous. He took her by the shoulders and kissed the top of her head, his lips brushing the ash-blonde hair he adored. Then he kissed her chastely on the forehead. "Goodbye, Ruth."

"Bye." She walked away from him without a wave or a backward glance.

Mayfield returned to his study and sat for a long time in his armchair with his eyes closed, his thoughts wandering through precious memories of the past . . . what she'd said . . . the clothes she'd worn . . . the things they had done together. He unlocked a drawer in his desk and took out his mementoes: notes written in a childish hand, birthday and Christmas cards from her—the kisses marked in large XXXs. There were the little presents she'd given him over the years which he'd carefully kept and never used: book marks, bars of soap, bottles of aftershave. He picked up the lock of hair he'd once cajoled from her and—like a lover—pressed it to his lips. Suddenly he swept all the souvenirs back into the drawer and locked it again. He couldn't bear to throw them away. Not yet.

Ordinarily there might have been some raised eyebrows in the village at a fourteen-year-old girl having a man of twenty-two for a boyfriend. Hughie Cole wasn't really a man though, he was more like a young boy. So nobody minded. Nobody except Ruth's brother Billy, that is.

"You're too young to go courting," he growled. "And I'm not allowing you out with that half-wit. I forbid it."

"*You* forbid it?" Ruth's eyes flashed. "You'd best tell Hughie then, hadn't you?" She knew he wouldn't. Billy hated Hugh but he was also afraid of him.

"I know what you're after, you randy little bitch!" Billy raved. "I'll beat the arse off you if you go with him!"

"You lay a finger on me, Billy, and Hugh will cripple you," she said witheringly. "He'll tear your head off."

Billy was beaten. Hugh Cole was a giant and he wasn't

right in the head. He could do something crazy if he lost his temper.

Under Ruth's influence Hugh Cole began to shave regularly and to comb his hair. People took a second look at him. Simple he might be, they murmured, but he wasn't at all bad-looking when he was smartened up.

No one knew what the Habenhowe twins thought. Billy Staton was their enemy but presumably they had nothing against his sister. Certainly they couldn't have been against the liaison or they would have stopped it. One word from them to Hughie and it would have been over.

TEN

Robert Oakleigh was secretly pleased to receive an invitation to Georgina and Georgette's sixteenth birthday party. The invitation, neatly hand-printed, dropped through the letterbox one evening. GEORGINA AND GEORGETTE HABENHOWE WOULD BE PLEASED IF ROBERT OAKLEIGH . . . He was half inclined to refuse. All their admirers would be there, vying with one another. Whenever he saw the twins now they always had one boy or another in tow. They seemed to make a point of parading their latest catch around the village like a prize bull with a ring through its nose. It would be churlish not to go to their party however, and besides, it might be amusing. Robert enjoyed a feeling of superiority that he had not been one of their conquests.

The party was held in the afternoon in a large room above the Black Dog. When Robert arrived, half the village seemed to be there already. Georgina and Georgette stood out unmistakably among the throng of people. They were dressed in pale lilac trouser suits with frilled shirts and large bow-tie to match. The colour set off their hair which shone like polished chestnut. Robert pushed his way through to them and handed over his present. They greeted him politely but coolly and passed him on to their mother. Gladys Habenhowe appeared pleased to see him but he was shocked at the change in her. She looked an old woman.

"How's your dad?" she asked.

"He's well, thank you, Mrs Habenhowe."

She nodded her head towards her daughters. "He delivered them, you know. Sixteen years ago today. Ten o'clock in the morning it was." She laid a hand on his arm. "Are you going to be a doctor like your dad?"

"Yes, I hope so."

"Wonderful thing, being a doctor." She leaned nearer. Her breath smelt of liquor. "Georgina was born first," she confided. "Georgette was ten minutes later." Her fingers dug into his arm. "A terrible time I had. Tore me something cruel they did, the pair of them." Robert shifted his feet uncomfortably, looking about him for a way of escape. Surely she didn't think he was interested in the details of her confinement? Gladys went on in a loud whisper: "Your dad had to stitch me up." Tearfully, she began fumbling in her bag. "Excuse me, I have to . . ." To his relief she drifted away from him. He watched her to the end of the room where she slipped furtively through a door.

Councillor Mayfield and his wife arrived. "Sweet sixteen and never been kissed, eh?" he said jovially, eyeing the twins with obvious relish. "We'll soon put that right!" However, as his mouth moved forward each girl in turn inclined her head at the last moment and adroitly intercepted his eager lips with her cheek. As he stood back from them the disappointment in Mayfield's face changed to wonderment. "You're both wearing name badges," he remarked in amazement.

It was something Robert had noticed with surprise too. Georgina and Georgette each wore a tiny brooch pinned to her lapel with her name on it.

A voice cackled in Robert's ear. Gladys Habenhowe had returned. "What he doesn't know is that every so often they go to the loo and swap brooches. It's one of their little jokes." The whisky fumes on her breath were heavier than ever. "Oh, you wouldn't believe the tricks those two can get up to." She gazed mournfully up at him. The whites of her eyes were an unhealthy yellow and were streaked with broken blood vessels.

Robert spotted Hugh Cole towering above everyone on the far side of the room. "Excuse me, Mrs Habenhowe, I must say hallo to Hughie."

She nodded vacantly. "Remember me to your dad."

When he reached Hugh he found Ruth Staton and Dolly Kronks standing with him.

"Don't the twins look simply beautiful," Ruth sighed, after they had been chatting for a while.

"Oh, *I* don't think so," Dolly said. "Attractive maybe— but that's only because of their clothes. They've learned dress-sense." Dolly, three years Ruth's senior, spoke patronisingly. She made eyes at Robert. "What do you think?"

He made a pretence of studying Georgina and Georgette

although he had formed his opinion earlier, when he arrived. He'd been taken aback. The twins had grown up. They were poised and sophisticated. Robert thought they were stunning.

"I think they're very elegant," he said.

He hadn't intended to stay to the end and when the cake had been cut and passed round, and the floor was being cleared for dancing, he went to bid farewell to Georgina and Georgette.

"You're not *going*?" They exchanged a look. "You can't. It's rude to leave this early."

He stared at them. Were they simply piqued that he was leaving or did they actually care? Their faces were composed as he searched for some clue to their real feelings. Their eyes were controlled and more knowing than when he'd last looked at them closely. That had been in the evenings they spent together in their hideout with Hughie. He'd lost the knack now of picking out Georgette by the way she looked at him—or else she no longer looked at him differently from her sister.

Awkwardly, he began to make excuses for leaving. The twins were adamant. "We want you to stay."

"Well, if you really do, then—"

"Let's start the dancing." They seized a hand each and dragged him to the centre of the floor. Somewhere at the back of the room a record-player started playing.

For the rest of the party Robert found himself alternating between Georgina and Georgette. Always he was in the company of one of them. "We're not letting you out of our sight," they told him. "You might try to slip away."

He was amused and flattered. For some reason he'd become the centre of their attention. It was very pleasant and he wallowed in the envious glances of the other boys. As the party progressed he was happy to discover a return of that vague quality in Georgette that so intrigued him. She was the tiniest degree more relaxed and yielding towards him than her sister. Georgina kept him at a slight distance all the time. They'd swapped their brooches twice during the party and each time he had realised it before very long.

During the last dance Georgette said: "You can walk us

home." It wasn't so much a suggestion as a command, but Robert didn't mind.

"I'd like to," he said, aware of the expectant faces of other boys who had stayed hopefully on to the end. He noticed Gladys Habenhowe slumped in a chair at the far end of the room. "What about your mother?" he asked dutifully.

"Don't mind her," Georgina said curtly. "She'll stay here until opening time."

At their weatherboard house in North Street the twins laughingly tugged Robert inside. He didn't think anything, even when Georgina put her back against the door and said:

"Got you at last, Robert Oakleigh."

"Aren't you lucky?" he joked cheerfully.

"So are you," Georgette told him. "It's your lucky day."

"Comes of being the doctor's son," said Georgina, reaching behind her and bolting the door.

Robert tensed. "What do you mean?"

Georgette's eyes were warm and glowing. "We want you to deflower us," she said.

"*What?*"

"Remove our virginity," said Georgina.

They were teasing, of course, having him on. Well, he could play that game too. "If you mean clinically, you'd better speak to my father."

"No, the natural method will do nicely, thank you." Georgette's mouth curved in a smile.

"You won't get into trouble," Georgina assured him. "We've reached the age of consent. Legally, we became sixteen at midnight last night."

Robert was eighteen and understood the mechanics of sex well enough but his practical experience to date had been negligible. He was certain that they were only baiting him, however. This was another of their tricks. He would play them along.

"O.K., where do you want me to perform and who's first?" he asked flippantly.

Georgina looked at Georgette. "Bo-bo?"

Georgette shook her head. "Zizzyplonk," she said.

It was then that Robert became unnerved. They'd

reverted to what he called "Twinspeak"—their own private language. He didn't know what "Zizzyplonk" meant but "Bo-bo" was bed. It was a relic of their baby talk and one of the few words he'd learned from playing with them in the past.

Georgette held out her hand to him. "On the couch," she said, "with me."

"Take your clothes off," Georgina ordered.

He'd attempted to call their bluff and failed. They were bent on making a fool of him . . . getting their own back because he hadn't fallen at their feet like other boys. He had to retreat with as much dignity as possible. "The joke has gone far enough," he said.

"Joke? What joke?" They moved towards him. "What's the matter, don't you fancy us?" One of them flicked out his tie.

"Perhaps he's scared," said Georgina.

"Or doesn't know how to do it," said Georgette.

"*Can't* do it, more likely," said Georgina.

"That's enough!" Robert snapped furiously, annoyed at the slight upon his virility. Angrily he hunted for a weak spot in their armour. He found one. "Anyway, you surprise me," he said casually. "From what I hear you both lost your virginity long ago."

That stopped their smiles. But their eyes told him he'd made a dreadful blunder. Before he could duck, his head was chopped from side to side as each girl delivered a stinging slap on the opposite cheek.

"I didn't mean—" he began.

"Out!" they shouted.

"I'm sorry, I—"

"*OUT!*" They opened the door and pushed him into the street. As he tried to apologise they slammed the door in his face.

Bewildered and upset, he walked home. Damn them! He would forget them from now on. Next month he started his degree course at university. He would only be in Tanniford at half-term and during vacations. He wouldn't be hurt by the sight of them gallivanting around the village any more. It was thoughts of Georgette that hurt the most. A new emotion had awakened in Robert when he held

Georgette in his arms at the party. It was a feeling he hadn't experienced before.

Justin Mayfield leaned forward to the mirror and studied his make-up. The dress rehearsal this evening had gone well. His performance in this play would be his best yet. Justin had been given a part in every school theatrical production since he joined the school. There was a dearth of boys willing to play girls' parts. Justin had no objection. He was always ready to dress up as a girl. It gave him an excuse to keep female clothing in his wardrobe at home. "I have to rehearse, you see," he explained to his mother. "It's quite difficult playing female parts." It wasn't for him, though, and he loved it.

"Aren't you ready to go yet, Mayfield?" A boy had put his head round the dressing-room door. His father had brought them to the rehearsal in his car.

"It's all right, I've arranged my own lift home," Justin said.

The boy withdrew. Justin stood up and admired his reflection in the mirror. The dress clung to his slim, thirteen-year-old's figure. His dark hair, carefully cut and styled, was immaculate. No wig had been necessary and with his smooth face he had been perfect in the play as an attractive girl of the Twenties. He turned and looked back over his shoulder, checking the stocking-seams and seeing if his slip was showing. Justin was a perfectionist. He dressed for the part completely, even to the silk undies. Satisfied, he stepped into the corridor and walked un hurriedly and—despite the high heels—without awkwardness to the door and out into the darkness.

Outside the school gates he paused and looked about him before sauntering towards the figure in crash helmet sitting astride a motorcycle.

"Thanks for coming Billy."

"That's O.K." Billy Staton's voice was gruff. He handed Justin a helmet and leather jacket. Justin put them on, then carefully hitched up his dress and mounted the pillion. Billy started the engine and Justin clutched him round the middle as, with a deafening roar, the bike shot away into the night.

Billy did not follow the nearest route to Tanniford but made a detour that took in a stretch of motorway. As they joined the motorway he opened the throttle wide. The speedometer climbed rapidly . . . 60 . . . 70 . . . 80. Billy's teeth parted in a grin as Justin's arms tightened around him. 90 . . . 100. The boy had wanted to feel what it was like to do a ton. Well, now he knew.

A quarter of an hour later they sped down the quiet High Street and parked the bike in Tanniford's tiny square. Justin had made no comment when they hurtled past his house at the top of hill. They took off their helmets and jackets.

"Let's take a walk," said Billy.

"Where?"

"In the churchyard."

"All right."

The iron gate screeched in the silence. "Over here," said Billy, steering Justin off the tarmac path and towards the dark shadow of the great holly tree in the corner.

Justin hesitated and stopped. "What's in there?"

"Nothing. Just an open space behind the tree. Didn't you ever play there as a kid?"

"No." Justin looked up at him and the faint moonlight made his eyes glisten. Billy caught the scent of perfume. He put his arm round the girlish waist. This was like pulling a bird . . . better, in fact. He began to sweat with excitement.

"Come on," he urged, gripping Justin's arm.

Justin's memories of what took place in the hidden corner of the churchyard were blurred with shame. The high-speed dash along the motorway had been terrifying. He'd wanted to scream with the thrill of it. He'd had the same feeling as Billy's grip hardened on his arm and he allowed himself to be pushed and dragged into the darkness behind the holly tree. There had been a trestle-table there—left behind after some church bazaar. He remembered the hardness of the wood against his face. Billy whispering: "Other way up . . . like a girl." His snigger. "Just in, Justin, just in." The smell of his sweat. The iron trestles rattling. Slinking home afterwards, soiled and degraded.

ELEVEN

Gladys Habenhowe died two years later. She was fifty-eight. "Cirrhosis," Dr Oakleigh wrote on the death certificate. "Drink," said the village, "that's what caused it. She drank herself to death." There were some who blamed the twins for their mother's death. It was her wild daughters, they said, and the worry they caused, that drove poor Gladys to drink and made her an alcoholic.

No one knew if Georgina and Georgette were upset by their mother's death or not. Outwardly they showed no signs of distress. They went into mourning and they wore black for the funeral but, as the Reverend Gaye noted during the service, neither of them shed a tear. Most eighteen-year-olds would have done. Perhaps they were better able to hide their feelings than other girls, he thought charitably.

Henry Mayfield received two visits the day after Gladys's funeral. Both of them were unexpected. The first visitor was Hugh's mother, Carol Cole. It gave Mayfield a shock when his wife came to his study and told him: "Mrs Cole is at the front door asking to see you." Her voice was hard. Marjorie Mayfield was aware that her husband had once had an affair with Carol but she had no idea how serious it had been or that Hugh had been the result.

Mayfield regarded Carol nervously as she entered the study and sat down. She had kept their bargain and never breathed a word to anyone about Hugh's paternity. What did she want now, after all this time?

"How are you, Carol?"

"I'm well, thank you." She came straight to the point. "It's about Hughie."

"Yes?"

"He's a man now. He's twenty-five. You know I've always done my best for him . . ." Her voice tailed away.

"Yes, you have," he assured her gently. "The boy couldn't have had a better mother."

"Thanks." She sniffed and pulled out a handkerchief. There were tears in her eyes. "It's not as if—" She stopped and blew her nose. "—as if he will ever be any different . . .

or lead a normal life."

"He had a girlfriend for a while though, didn't he?" Mayfield kept his tone neutral.

"Young Ruth Staton, you mean? Yes." Carol smiled sadly. "He was so proud of her. She was very sweet to him, I believe, but nothing came of it. Well, nothing could really, could it?"

"No, I suppose not."

"She's grown up now. Pretty girl." Carol toyed with her handkerchief. "About Hugh, though. The thing is . . . he and his stepfather don't get on any more. It was all right when Hugh was a boy but he's a man now—whatever his brain's like—and Lionel says he won't put up with him any longer." She went on hurriedly: "I can see it from his side. When he married me he didn't know Hugh would turn out like he has—none of us did, of course. Hugh's not easy to live with . . . and he doesn't like Lionel." She looked down at her hands. "Lionel says either Hugh goes or *he* will. I don't know what to do," she ended miserably.

"What about a larger house?" Mayfield suggested.

She shook her head. "It wouldn't be any good. Lionel won't have him in the same house. He wants me to have Hugh put away. I *can't* do that. Anyway, he's not bad enough . . . they wouldn't take him." She raised her eyes. "I thought . . . with all your connections . . . you might be able to find somewhere for Hugh. Surely someone would be willing to take him as a lodger?"

"I'll see what I can do," he assured her. "Now, don't worry. I'll work out something."

The second visit that morning was from the Habenhowe twins. Mayfield thought how *chic* they looked in black as they sat on the edge of his sofa, their black-nyloned legs neatly crossed the same way. They seemed so demure in little pill-box hats with a veil that barely covered their foreheads that he found it hard to credit their notorious reputations as village hoydens.

"And what can your old godfather do for you, my dears?" he asked jocularly.

"We don't like our house."

"Oh-h, I see." Pert little minxes coming straight out with it like that and their mother not yet cold in her grave.

"We want to move out of the village."

"Really? And no doubt you've already decided where you'd like to go?" He couldn't refrain from sarcasm.

"Yes, as a matter of fact we have," one of them said sweetly. "It's a nice little house in its own grounds."

"At the top of Pilcox Hill," said the other, "and it's standing empty."

He knew the house they meant. Pilcox Cottage. He owned it. He'd been holding out for a good price.

"It belongs to you. You can sell it to us."

So they knew. "Yes, but hold on, I—"

"There's plenty of money in our Trust Fund." They smiled at him. "Mother explained all about the Trust Fund to us before she died."

How much had Gladys told them, he wondered. Everything, probably. There was no end to what Gladys might say when she was in her cups. Cautiously, he met their eyes. They were the eyes of Gladys Habenhowe as he remembered them years ago when she too had come to his house and made demands. Only now there were *two* pairs of Gladys's eyes fastened upon him.

Inwardly, he seethed. It was unfair. These two girls had more money than ever and they hadn't done a thing to deserve it. It was thanks to *him* they were so well off. He was the one who had taken out the insurances on their behalf against the death of their parents. Who would have thought they would lose their father *and* their mother by the time they were eighteen? And now they were after Pilcox Cottage. He was blowed if he would let them have it. The place would do for Hughie if only someone could— Henry Mayfield had a sudden inspiration.

"Pilcox Cottage is very isolated. I don't think two young girls should be up there all alone," he said doubtfully. "But I'll tell you what," he went on cunningly, "Hugh Cole's stepfather is turning him out. I promised his mother I'd find Hughie a place to live. I'd be willing to sell the house to you if you'd have Hughie as a lodger. After all, you're good friends and he's lived next door to you ever since you were born."

They looked at each other. "We wouldn't mind except the house is too small."

"I'll have an extension built," he offered quickly.

Again they looked at each other. They shook their heads and his hopes sank. Then one of them said:

"A caravan in the garden would be better for Hughie. There's plenty of room."

"That way we could have our privacy," said the other.

"It's a deal," he agreed. "I'll arrange everything." He noticed they showed no surprise at his concern for Hugh. Maybe they had learned the truth about him from their mother.

Thus it was that a month after Gladys Habenhowe died her twin daughters moved out of the house in North Street where they had lived all their lives and into the house at the top of Pilcox Hill. The following week a new caravan was delivered there and Hugh Cole was installed in it.

Whether out of respect for their mother's death, or because they had become bored with flirting and philandering, the twins would have nothing further to do with the local lads after their move to Pilcox Hill. The affairs stopped completely. A few admirers tried calling at Pilcox Cottage but they were given short shrift and Hugh Cole was there to see them off if they became persistent. One or two of the affronted would-be wooers made lewd suggestions to explain the rejection of their manly charms. "Big Hughie serves the two of them," they said with a leer. Or, "Those girls don't need a man . . . they see to each other."

Georgina and Georgette had joined the College of Art in the county town eight miles away when they left school and sometimes they were seen riding there on their mopeds. Very occasionally they descended into Tanniford to do some shopping but most times they sent Hugh down on his bicycle with notes to the shopkeepers telling them what they wanted delivered.

Despite their withdrawal from village life the Habenhowe twins did show up at the annual fete the following summer. In fact, they were one of the star attractions. The fete was in aid of the Mentally Handicapped and Mrs Mayfield congratulated herself on having pressed even those difficult Habenhowe girls into service. The lever she had used in their case was Hugh Cole.

"We're trying to assist lots of others like Hughie," she

cooed persuasively and at once they had agreed to help.
They said they would plan their own booth and devise
their own scheme for raising money and Marjorie Mayfield
departed feeling pleased at having recruited them. She
wasn't so pleased when she learned what their sideshow
comprised although she had to agree that it certainly
proved to be a money-spinner.

As usual the fete took place in the grounds of Mayfield
Hall. Robert Oakleigh and a fellow-student, Len Stewart,
who was spending a week's holiday with him, were among
the first to arrive. Apart from an occasional fleeting visit,
Robert hadn't spent any time in Tanniford since he had
started at university two years ago. On previous vacations
he had hitch-hiked around Europe relaxing from the grind
of his medical studies and deliberately cutting adrift from
Tanniford and his old roots for a while. He'd enjoyed the
freedom and companionship at university and found the
life there new and exciting. This summer however, to his
amazement, he'd felt homesick. There had been an urge to
return home . . . a need to renew the links with his background.

His friend, Len, came from a London suburb and loathed
it. He was mad about the countryside and what he described as "rural life" which, so far as Robert could discover,
meant anything that took place outside towns and cities.
Len had been overjoyed when Robert invited him to stay
with him in Tanniford for a week.

As they strolled around the fete Robert nodded to people
he knew and exchanged greetings with them. "That's
what I love about the country," Len said enthusiastically.
"Everybody knows everybody."

Robert laughed. "That works both ways. It also means
you can't do a damned thing here without everyone knowing about it."

A huge placard on poles on the other side of the field
caught their attention. WIN A KISS, it read.

"Sounds interesting. Let's see what it is," Len
suggested.

Beneath the sign when they reached it there was a small
stage around which a crowd was gathered. There were
barriers in front of the stage which kept the crowd at a

distance. As they approached, Robert recognised the two
figures on the stage who were attracting so much attention
and his eyes widened in astonishment.

Georgina and Georgette were dressed as Arabian slave-
girls. Yashmaks covered the lower half of their faces and
they wore limpid, ankle-length, harem trousers. As they
moved, the pellucid material undulated tantalisingly,
now hiding, now revealing, the nakedness beneath.

"Very fetching," Len murmured as he caught sight of
them. "Very fetching *indeed!*" He craned forward. "And
they look absolutely alike."

"They are. You're looking at Tanniford's identical
twins."

"Getaway! The girls you're always telling me about?"
Len gazed at them with interest.

Wally Kronks was acting as the barker. "Roll up! Roll
up! Roll up, my lucky lads!" he bawled. "Only a pound to
enter the arena for a really close look at these lovely
slaves. *And* there's a chance to win a kiss from one of them.
All the money goes to charity. Come along now! One at a
time, *if* you please."

The idea was simple. One twin wore a red bangle on her
wrist and, as Wally explained with a chuckle, all you had
to do was to make sure you knew which girl it was. You
paid your pound and went to the foot of the stage. The girls
executed a few belly-wobbles and danced about to taped
music during which they passed behind a screen on the
stage and emerged with their hands behind them. If you
could pick out the one wearing the bangle the girls twirled
around and danced behind the screen and out again. If you
identified the girl a second time you received a kiss.

"The odds are four to one against being right twice
running," Len said.

"Assuming there's no skill involved and it's entirely a
matter of chance," Robert pointed out.

"Well, it has to be unless there is some way of telling one
girl from the other."

They watched one contestant after another fail to win a
kiss. Then a middle-aged man was lucky. He clambered
eagerly on to the low platform, bent on claiming his
reward. The twins ran about in mock terror, dodging and

twisting and evading his clutching hands to the delight of the crowd. Finally one girl stood still and raised her yashmak. There was clapping and laughter as the man, panting with exertion, at last obtained his kiss.

Wally Kronks noticed Robert Oakleigh in the audience. "Come along young Robert," he shouted. "Have a go. It's for a good cause."

Singled out in that way, Robert felt unable to refuse. He handed Wally a pound, ducked under the barrier and approached the stage to face the twins.

"Well, if it isn't handsome Robert Oakleigh come to try his luck," one of them said. "Fancy your chances, do you?"

He glanced quickly at the girl who had spoken. All he would have to go on would be the expression in their eyes. Could he still tell?

"Had a good look, have you?" the same girl asked rudely.

Georgina. He was sure that was Georgina. Georgette was wearing the bracelet. He nodded. "Yes, thank you."

The music started and they enacted a dance in perfect unison. After they'd scampered behind the screen and out again, Robert studied what he could see of their faces as they stood clasping their hands behind them. He *hadn't* lost his skill. He pointed to Georgette and she brought her arms forward and displayed the bangle. There wasn't much reaction from the onlookers because he'd had a fifty-fifty chance of being right anyway and plenty of people chose correctly the first time.

The music started again and the girls repeated their performance. When Robert picked out Georgette a second time there was a burst of applause. He'd won a kiss.

"I'm not going to chase about after you," he warned as he leapt nimbly on to the stage.

"Who said we'd run away?" Georgette removed her yashmak and offered her mouth to him. Robert gripped her shoulders and kissed her warmly to the accompaniment of wolf-whistles and catcalls from the spectators. She smiled slightly as he released her.

"There you are, gents," Wally boomed, quick to capitalise on the situation. "See how easy it is? Come along now, who'll be the next lucky lad?"

"I'd like another go," Robert called out, jumping down

from the platform. He wanted to kiss that soft mouth again and it struck him that this was a very pleasant way of paying the twins out for the time they'd made a fool of him after their sixteenth birthday party.

Wally guffawed. "Well, well, well!" he roared, playing to the crowd. "That says something for the young lady's kisses! Good luck to you, sir!" He stepped forward and accepted another pound note from Robert.

The pantomime began again. It was easy for Robert now. Although Georgina had her expression firmly under control she was unable to hide the annoyance in her eyes. There were exclamations of surprise and a ripple of applause as he once more picked out Georgette on the first round. "That's amazing," someone said. Georgina's eyes were hostile. The second time the twins seemed slightly longer in coming from behind the screen. Confidently, Robert pointed to Georgette. He was flabbergasted when she brought her hands to the front and he saw that her wrist was bare. Georgina stepped forward, her eyes triumphant, and threw her arms in the air with a flourish. There, on her wrist, was the red bangle.

The crowd muttered with disappointment. "Oh, bad luck, bad luck!" Wally cried. "We can't win every time though. Who's next?"

Robert stared at Georgette. She avoided his eyes. He made a gesture of resignation and pushed his way through the spectators to rejoin Len Stewart.

"Never mind," Len said sympathetically. "You did jolly well. The odds were sixten to one against you doing it four times running."

"Damn the odds!" Robert snapped angrily. "They cheated!"

"You mean you *can* see a difference between them?"

"Sometimes. Just about."

"So, somehow they twigged that you knew and they transferred the bracelet during the few seconds they were behind the screen?"

"They must have done," Robert said sulkily.

His friend laughed uproariously. "Oh, Robert, old son, you should see your face! It was only a bit of fun. Where's your sense of humour?"

Robert's face broke into a grin. "Blast their eyes!" he said cheerfully. "I wanted another kiss."

"I'd sure like to meet those girls, Len said. "You know them. Can't you introduce me?"

Robert pursed his lips. Then, "Yes, O.K." he said. "I'll ask Wally what time they're taking a break."

TWELVE

Robert Oakleigh and his friend returned to the WIN A KISS site at midday when Wally Kronks had told them the twins would be taking a half-hour rest. Georgina and Georgette were sitting cross-legged on the grass behind the stage eating sandwiches. Hugh Cole squatted beside them.

"Who's the boyfriend?" Len asked as they walked towards the group.

"He's not a boyfriend, he just lives with them," said Robert and then laughed at the comic expression on his friend's face. "No, I don't mean it the way you think. That's Hughie. He's a bit simple. He lives in a caravan in the garden of their house. He's always around . . . a sort of guard dog."

"He's massive. I shouldn't like to tangle with him," Len said.

"He's quite harmless unless he thinks you're hurting the twins."

"Those girls are very dishy," Len said. They were still out of earshot. "I'm going to ask one of them for a date."

Robert had it on the tip of his tongue to warn him that Georgina and Georgette didn't accept a date for one and that he'd have to invite both of them out. But for all he knew the twins had changed.

Hugh had a chicken leg between his hands and was tearing at it with his teeth. He looked up without taking it from his mouth as they approached. Robert was reminded of a dog with a bone.

"Hullo, Hughie." Hugh jerked his head in acknowledgement and continued gnawing. Robert turned to the girls. "This is Leonard Stewart. He's a friend of mine from college and he'd like to meet you."

Two pairs of hands were daintily wiped on two paper serviettes. They came to their feet and politely shook hands.

"I'm Georgina . . ."

". . . and I'm Georgette."

"I saw your act. I think it's great," Len told Georgina.

"Actually, I'm rather interested in Probability and the Laws of Chance. Now, do you realise that . . ."

Robert watched with amusement as Len engaged Georgina in earnest conversation and skilfully edged her to one side.

"You owe me a kiss, you know," Robert said to Georgette. "You cheated that last time."

"You were cheating too," she said spiritedly, "because you *knew* which was me. How *did* you know?" she asked curiously. "Was there a mark on my outfit or something? We took such care."

"It was pure luck," he lied.

Len Stewart's quiet conversation with Georgina suddenly became public as she said loudly: "We don't go out without each other."

"You want your sister to come too? That's O.K." Len said. "I'll bring a partner."

Georgette spoke up. "No thanks. We don't make four-somes." Len's face was perplexed. "Of course," she went on, "we *might* make an exception. It would depend who the other person was."

He's walking right into this, thought Robert. They know he'll suggest me and they're just waiting to shriek: "Oh no! Not that dreadful Robert Oakleigh!" He began composing a suitable retort as he heard Len say, "It would be Robert, of course."

"Oh, *that's* all right then," he was amazed to hear Georgette reply. "Robert's an old friend of ours . . . a very old friend." He waited for the catch, the sting in the tail. The twist, the barb. He knew them of old. But none came. He turned and looked at Georgette. Her smile was friendly. He brightened. They *had* changed. He returned her smile.

"That's settled then," Len said. "Pick you up at seven o'clock."

It was a warm evening as Len drove his battered old Lancia up Pilcox Hill. "I've never met identical twins before," he told Robert. "You used to know them pretty well. What are they like?"

"In a word . . . *unpredictable*," said Robert.

His friend grinned. "I think they're absolutely fascinating."

"Just treat them like any other girls. *Don't* ask them
what it's like being identical twins. They've been bored
stiff by people's curiosity since they were old enough to
talk."

"I'll remember," Len promised.

Pilcox Cottage stood on its own at the end of a lane
leading from the crest of Pilcox Hill. The house had been
built at the turn of the century by an eccentric shipowner
who hankered for splendid views and for isolation from his
fellow-men. The site had provided both and still did. There
were no other houses nearer than half a mile. The rear of
the house faced rolling open country and the front looked
out over the river valley and Tanniford village.

As the Lancia bumped and groaned along the unmade
track towards the house Hugh Cole came out of the door of
his caravan.

"I say, he really is like a guard dog," Len commented as
Hugh bounded to the front gate and stood hanging over it
watching their approach.

Georgina and Georgette emerged from the front door of
the house. As they did so the evening sun caught their
hair, making it gleam a dark golden colour. They wore
white, low-backed summer dresses and gold, open-toed
sandals. Each girl wore her name in fancy gold letters
hanging from a chain round her neck. Hugh Cole opened
the gate for them and they tripped gaily down the path and
out to the car.

"What would you like to do?" Len asked as they clambered in. "Shall we drive out to a country pub for a few
drinks first and then have a meal at a restaurant?"

"We'd prefer fish-and-chips on the beach," Georgette
said.

"With cans of beer," Georgina added.

Len's face was a study. He'd had in mind a posh restaurant and waiters.

"There's a fish-and-chip shop on the way to the beach,"
Georgette told him.

"And an off-licence near the seafront," said Georgina.

Len looked at Robert, his eyebrows raised question-
ingly. Robert nodded. "Suits me," he said, "but it's about

twenty miles to the coast. I'll direct you."

An hour later they sat on the beach watching the sun go down. The newspaper-wrapped fish and chips had been put inside a plastic bag and double-wrapped in the car blanket to keep them hot. Len had parked the car at the end of the small promenade and they had walked to a deserted part of the beach at the foot of a low cliff.

"Use your fingers," Georgina advised as Len poked ineffectually at his fried fish with one of the tiny plastic forks supplied by the fish shop.

"This was a great idea of yours," Len said, abandoning table-manners and pushing a piece of fish into his mouth with finger and thumb. "I'm really enjoying myself."

"Good. So are we." Georgina wiped her hands on a sheet of newspaper and pulled the ring-top on a can of beer.

Robert met Georgette's eyes. "Me too," he whispered. She smiled and lightly squeezed his arm. Out at sea a lone yacht glided past the landfall buoy and changed course on a fresh tack.

"Let's stroll along the water's edge," Len suggested later, when they had finished eating.

Behind them the promenade lights glowed in the twilight. The only sounds around them were made by the waves of a calm sea as they rasped back and forth over the sand. Len and Georgina walked ahead arm-in-arm and Robert noticed that Len kept gently urging Georgina forward so as to increase the distance away from Georgette and himself. Robert tried to co-operate by slowing down Georgette but when he did so Georgina slowed down Len as well so that the distance remained constant.

After a while Len said in exasperation, "Are you two girls joined together with invisible rope or something?" He pointed into the gloom ahead. "I'll bet you couldn't walk to that breakwater with me and leave your sister here with Robert."

"Don't be silly," Georgina said. "Of course I can." She began walking.

Robert guided Georgette towards some beach huts and drew her into the darkness between two of them. "You still owe me a kiss," he reminded her.

She uttered a little laugh and raised her head to shout:

"Georgie? Robert says I owe him a kiss."

Georgina's voice floated back on the night air. "Then give it to him Georgie dear. We must pay our debts, mustn't we?"

Georgette tilted her face up. Robert bent his head and closed his mouth over hers. He felt Georgette yielding. Her arms slid round his neck and her lips opened in a long, deep kiss. He was surprised and exhilarated; he hadn't expected her to be so responsive. The kiss stretched into several more. Robert leaned back against a beach hut with his arms encircling Georgette's waist and pulling her close. His hands touched bare flesh above the low back of her dress and he stroked his fingers upwards over her skin to her neck. She gave a little shiver and wriggled against him.

"I wonder how Len's getting along with Gina," he murmured.

"Not very well," she mumbled into his chest. "At least, not as well as he'd like to, I think."

He wondered if she spoke from foreknowledge or from that extra-sensory perception of each other's feelings that she and Georgina seemed to possess.

"Unlucky Len," he whispered, putting a hand under her chin and lifting her face. "Lucky me." His lips returned to her soft, warm mouth.

"And me." She spoke into his open mouth and her hands ruffled the hair at the back of his head.

Some time later they heard the voices of Len and Georgina approaching. Georgette pulled her mouth away in the middle of a kiss. "Time to go," she said.

"Blast!" Robert said vehemently. Why couldn't Len have kept Georgina occupied a while longer? Robert envied his friend's confidence and success with girls. At college Len would walk up to a strange girl at any kind of gathering and talk her into going out with him. Usually, soon after, he'd talk her into bed.

As Robert and Georgette emerged from between the huts, Georgina and Len were walking towards them. "Time to go," Georgina said crisply, repeating Georgette's words. "It's late."

Robert glanced at Len. It was difficult to see his expression in the dark but Robert thought he looked glum.

In the car on the way home to Tanniford Georgina and Georgette chatted happily but Len seemed subdued. "They might at least have invited us in for coffee," he said gloomily as he drove down Pilcox Hill after dropping the twins at their house.

"I'm not surprised they didn't," Robert said. "They're very . . ." He tried to think of a suitable word. ". . . *private* is the only way I can describe them."

"You can say that again!" his friend said with feeling.

"Oh? How did you make out with Gina?"

"O.K. up to a point. I mean, she was friendly and we necked and kissed. She wouldn't *give* though."

"You can't expect every girl you meet to surrender first time."

"It wasn't that. She'd decided exactly how far she would go—as though she'd worked everything out beforehand. She gave just enough . . . enough anaesthetic, as it were . . . to put me under. It was like being kept under sedation."

Robert laughed. "What an imagination! All because she didn't fall for your routine. You weren't her type, that's all."

"I don't think anyone is," Len said gloomily. "That Georgina is definitely spooky, if you ask me. What about your one? How was Georgette?"

"So-so," Robert said non-commitally. He didn't want to discuss Georgette with Len. Nor to mention that when he'd kissed her goodnight she'd invited him to tea at the weekend when Len's stay in Tanniford would be over.

Len turned the car into Ferry Street and parked outside Robert's house. As he switched off the engine he said thoughtfully: "I had the oddest feeling when I was with Georgina at the breakwater. I had the feeling that you and I had been manipulated. I know I was the one who asked for the date, but I'm certain it was *you* they were really interested in."

THIRTEEN

Tea on the following Saturday afternoon seemed a strangely old-fashioned affair to Robert. Georgina and Georgette might have been two well-brought-up Victorian girls entertaining a gentleman visitor. Hugh Cole was there, hovering in the background—much as an older brother might have chaperoned his sisters. There was thin bread and butter, strawberry jam and slices of home-made cake. Tea was poured from a silver teapot with ornamental feet.

Tea was served in the front room. One of the walls was hung with pictures of local scenes which had been painted by Georgina and Georgette. "Our masterpieces," they told him laughingly. He stared at the pictures wishing he understood more about art so that he could have seen if the twins revealed any differences in their paintings.

Afterwards it occurred to Robert that the tea-time conversation had been mainly about his family background and his relatives, which was surprising since Georgina and Georgette had not shown the slightest interest before. Perhaps, like good hostesses, they were merely being polite to a guest in talking about him and not about themselves. It was odd though—almost as if they were checking his pedigree . . . assessing him.

He kissed Georgette goodbye at the gate as he left and she came readily into his arms. "When may I see you again?" he asked.

"Tomorrow, if you like. We'll be going down by the river to paint as usual. Why not come with us? We take a picnic lunch."

"I'd love to. I'll bring a bottle of wine and some cheeses."

"That would be nice." She offered her mouth a second time and he kissed her greedily.

Robert was cheerful as he walked home down the hill. It was good to be friends again. Well, friends with Georgina—a good deal more than that with Georgette. She had never quite faded from his memory while he'd been away. She'd had a habit of popping up in his thoughts—usually when he was out with other girls at college.

The next two weeks fell into a pattern. It was August and the weather was warm and dry. Each morning he set off along the old disused branch of the railway line from Tanniford and met Georgina and Georgette where the line joined the riverbank and ran alongside the river. It was near here that the twins had had their hideout years ago. Robert walked to the place one morning while he was waiting. The archway was empty and neglected and it smelt of damp. No village children made use of it now.

Georgina and Georgette would ride down to the meeting place on their mopeds, bumping over a rough track across the fields. Hugh Cole followed, not far behind, on his push-bike. Georgette told Robert they had tried to teach Hugh to ride a moped but he couldn't co-ordinate the controls properly. Neither could he master the Highway Code, so he wouldn't have been able to pass the test and obtain a licence anyway.

The girls, usually in open-necked shirts and jeans, would set up their easels on the riverbank near the mouth of a small creek. Across the entrance was the skeleton of an iron bridge which had once carried the branch line over the water. The rusting remains sticking up out of the mud formed the subject of their latest painting. Hugh pottered around the edge of the water and Robert lay on his back revising his pathology notes or reading a book.

"Robert . . . do you actually *examine* people yet? You know . . . girls?" Georgette asked one morning. She was mixing colours vigorously on her palette. Her voice was full of curiosity.

He laughed and sat up. "Only cadavers . . . dead ones. They don't let us loose on live patients until we've passed our second M.B. next year."

"How morbid." She shuddered. "Handling dead bodies, I mean."

"Not really. You become used to it."

Most days, after lunch they would walk to the head od the creek and back to stretch their legs. Hugh was left behind to guard their things. There would be another two or three hours work in the afternoon and then the four of them would ride home to Pilcox Hill. Robert rode pillion on Georgette's moped, clutching her easel under one arm, his

other arm round her waist; and Hugh puffed along behind
on his bike carrying the rest of their gear in a large
haversack slung across his shoulders.

The evening too fell into a routine. Robert invariably
stayed on at Pilcox Cottage until ten or eleven o'clock.

"Not eating with us any more?" his father asked
jokingly at the end of the first week.

"Robert, you must invite those girls back here to
dinner," his mother urged. "It's only right."

"I already have. They won't come," he told her. "Oh, it's
nothing to do with you . . . us," he added hastily, seeing the
pained expression on his mother's face. "They're just not
very sociable."

Mrs Oakleigh sighed. "This reminds me of when you
were children. They hardly ever came to the house then
either. You used to go off with them and I never knew
where you were. Such strange girls." She gave him a
searching look. "They are *nice* girls, aren't they, Robert?
And there's no need to smile at me like that! There were
some dreadful tales about them at one time."

"They are *very* nice girls, mother," he said firmly.

"And what about your studying?" Dr Oakleigh
demanded. "You won't find you can walk through your
M.B. It takes a lot of hard effort."

"I'm working well." Robert told him. "Much better than
I would do at home, in fact."

It was true. The evenings at the cottage were peaceful
and quiet. Georgina and Georgette were each engaged on a
large embroidery. They spoke very little but the
atmosphere was companionable and pleasant. Robert
didn't find the long silences the least bit uncomfortable as
he sat at a table revising and writing up his notes. He
disliked talkative girls. One girl at college had talked
non-stop from the moment he picked her up at her lodgings
to the moment an hour later when, in desperation, he'd
stopped her mouth with a kiss. Even so she had gone on
chattering between kisses, treating them—and love-
making—as no more than temporary interruptions to the
flow of her words.

At the beginning of September his parents went abroad
for a month's holiday. Robert did not go with them. The

original plan had been for him to stay with his friend Len
Stewart in London. Robert had not relished the idea of
being cooped up in a small semi in surburban London for
four weeks of summer. He'd mentioned the fact to the
twins.

"Why not stay in Tanniford," they suggested. "You can
eat with us. Then you need only go home to sleep. If you
feel thingish about if you can bring your own food."

"Are you sure you can manage here on your own?" his
mother asked anxiously when he told her he wasn't going
to London after all.

"Of course he can!" his father said. "Stop treating him
like an adolescent—he's nearly twenty-two."

Dr and Mrs Oakleigh departed early on a Saturday
morning. That evening at Pilcox Cottage, as Robert began
collecting his books together preparatory to returning
home, Georgina looked up from her embroidery frame and
said casually:

"You don't want to go back to an empty house, do you
Robert? Why not stay here. We have a spare bedroom."

He gaped at her in astonishment. Georgette was bent
over her own embroidery carefully concentrating on her
stitching.

"Thank you. I'd like to, if it's not too much trouble. An
empty house *is* rather depressing."

"No trouble. I'll see to the bed, then."

As Georgina left the room Georgette jumped up and
came and sat on his lap. Her mouth sought his. Robert
closed his arms round her with a sigh of contentment.

When Georgina came downstairs again Georgette continued to sit on his lap with her arms round his neck,
kissing him. Georgina sat down at her embroidery frame.

"Hughie will lend you a razor in the morning," she said,
resuming her work.

Sometime later she yawned and said: "It's Sunday
tomorrow. We always have a lie-in on Sundays. Shall we
say ten o'clock for breakfast?"

"Yes, fine," Robert replied over the top of Georgette's
head.

He went to bed feeling bewildered. He couldn't understand Georgina's attitude. She had acted as though it was

quite usual for her sister to be sitting on his lap petting and caressing. Her occasional glances had been approving . . . warm . . . as though she was sharing an experience with them.

There were only two bedrooms upstairs. The small one allotted to him and a larger one shared by Georgina and Georgette. Soon after he'd turned out the light and gone to bed the door of his room opened.

"I came to see if you were comfortable." He switched on the bedside light. Georgette stood beside his bed completely naked. He stared at her for a long moment then held out his hand. She made no protest as he drew her into bed beside him.

"Be gentle," she whispered. "Please . . . be very gentle." He nodded, unable to speak for emotion.

Georgette was a virgin. He was surprised and then ashamed of himself for being surprised. And he had no right to be so pleased about it, but he was.

The next morning at breakfast Georgina said: "Wouldn't it be simpler if you stayed here all the time your parents are away? I mean, what's the point of going home every night? Unless you want to, of course."

He looked at Georgette. She was smiling and her eyes were soft.

"Yes, well thank you. I'd like that very much."

He lived those weeks in the little house on Pilcox Hill in a dream. Every night Georgette came to his bed and every morning the three of them sat down to breakfast as though it was all perfectly normal. Robert felt he'd fallen under a spell. The situation was unreal . . . a kind of paradise cut off from the rest of the world.

One evening when he was sitting in an armchair in the front room reading, the door behind him had opened and the light had been switched off. With a rustle of clothing she had flopped into his lap and her arms had enfolded him.

"Darling . . ." she breathed. "I want you . . ."

He responded eagerly and for several minutes he fondled and caressed her, exulting in her abandon. "Oh, Georgette . . ."

With an explosive snort of laughter she broke from him,

ran to the door and switched on the light.

"Wrong! Wrong! Wrong!" It was Georgina dancing round the room with delight. "I *told* you he can't really tell, Georgie."

Georgette appeared in the doorway. She too was laughing.

"That wasn't particularly clever," Robert said crossly. "It's easy to pretend to be someone else in the dark."

"You were *convinced*, Robert." Georgina's eyes were glowing.

He had been too. Absolutely. She'd been acting, of course, but he was shaken all the same. He'd been completely taken in.

In bed that night Georgette chided him for being angry with Georgina.

"I should have thought you would be too," he said silkily. "She was responding just like you."

"Well, what else did you expect?" She gurgled with laughter.

"Don't you *mind*?"

"No, of course not." She sounded genuinely surprised by the question.

"Perhaps you wouldn't even care if I went to bed with her," Robert suggested provocatively. To his annoyance she giggled and replied promptly: "No, I shouldn't mind at all."

He was silent for a while, not sure whether to be angry or amused.

"Do you like my body?" she asked.

"I adore it," he said muzzling her breast with his face.

"It's exactly the same as Gina's, you know. We once spent a whole day exploring every inch of each other to see if we could find any difference. There wasn't so much as a pimple."

"Interesting," he murmured, not knowing what else to say and being more interested in his own explorations at the moment.

She checked his roving hand. "So I wonder why you prefer me. I mean, suppose Gina came into bed with you in the dark tomorrow night—how would you know it wasn't me?"

"Because . . ." He floundered, then grasped at a way out. "It would be like the first time with you."

"Not if it wasn't *her* first time, it wouldn't."

"Well, I'd just know," he said defensively.

"No, you wouldn't. For all you know it could have been Gina and not me on any of the nights you've been here."

"Stop it!" he said angrily. He sat up in bed and switched on the light. She glanced at his face and burst out laughing. "Poor Robert, you look as though you've been hit over the head."

"I don't understand you and Georgina," he said gloomily.

She stopped laughing. "No, my love," she said soberly, "I know you don't. Nobody does." She rolled over on top of him and kissed his nose. "Make love to me, Robert darling," she whispered.

A night or two later, when Georgette was kneeling over him moving urgently and moaning with pleasure, he happened to look towards the door of the bedroom. Although the room was in darkness he could see that it stood partly open whereas he was certain he had closed it earlier. His body began responding to Georgette's insistent rhythm and he surrendered control and was lost for a while in throbbing ecstasy. At the peak of her orgasm Georgette cried out with delight and at the same moment Robert thought he heard a corresponding cry from outside the door.

He thought the same thing happened on other nights; but he no longer cared about anything except the continuation of his nightly trip to paradise. By the end of the month he was deeply in love with Georgette Habenhowe. He made the mistake of believing she loved him in return.

His parents returned from holiday the day before the new term started. He was packing his bags when his father knocked on the door of his room and entered.

"My locum tells me he hasn't seen hair or hide of you while we've been away, Robert." His tone was questioning.

"Er-no, I didn't look in on the surgery at all I'm afraid. I'm sorry. Was everything all right?"

"Yes, as it happens. But you weren't in the house either, apparently."

Robert met his father's gaze frankly. "The Habenhowe twins invited me to stay with them. I accepted."

"I see." Dr Oakleigh uttered a heavy sigh. "Well, I suppose you're old enough to know what you're doing."

"Yes, I am."

His father looked at him keenly. "Where's this leading, Robert?"

"I don't know that it's leading anywhere. I'm just happy being with them, that's all."

"Oh, come now, Robert," Dr Oakleigh said sharply. "Even in these permissive days you don't live in a house for a month with two girls unless there's something more to it."

"All right. I'm in love with Georgette. Does that satisfy you?"

Dr Oakleigh asked quietly: "And is she in love with you?"

Robert hesitated. "She hasn't actually said so but yes, I think she is."

His father moved to the doorway apparently lost in thought. He turned after a while. "Do they pack in much genetics on your course?"

"Quite a bit."

"You realise, of course, that the Habenhowe twins are monozygotic?"

"Yes."

"But do you understand the implications? Especially in their case?"

"What do you mean by 'especially in their case'?"

"The circumstances of their birth, for one thing. I'll spare you the obstetric details but take it from me they became two foetuses only at the last possible stage. Any later and they would have been conjoined . . . Siamese twins."

Robert laughed nervously. "You make them sound like freaks."

His father said gravely. "They *are* freaks, Robert. Freaks of nature."

"They're not!" Robert said hotly.

Dr Oakleigh continued unperturbed. "Their other handicap is the way they were brought up. Their mother wouldn't take my advice and by the time she realised she was wrong it was too late. There is no chance of those girls leading normal lives now."

"I don't believe that!"

"Don't you? Then consider this," his father went on calmly. "The genetic bond between monozygotic twins is like nothing else in the world. It is closer than any other relationship. A mother and child have half their genes in common. Georgina and Georgette have *all* their genes in common. They have exactly the same genes . . . the same blood circulates in their bodies . . . the same—"

"All right! I accept all that but I don't see that it matters so much."

"You don't understand, do you?" Dr Oakleigh shook his head wonderingly. "Listen to me. Do you really imagine they could live separately from each other now? Or that they would let anyone or anything come between them? Marriage, for instance?"

"I don't want to hear any more of this," Robert said desperately.

"I'm only telling you for your own good, Robert," his father said gently. "You'll be the one who will be hurt, not either of them."

"Is anything the matter?" Georgette asked when he went to the cottage to say goodbye on his return to university the next day.

"No, why?"

"Because you look so sad," said her sister.

He forced a weak smile. "That's because I shan't see you again until the end of term," he said. "It's too far to come down and back in a weekend. Will you write to me?"

"Yes, we'll write." It was Georgina who answered.

FOURTEEN

No one in Tanniford was absolutely certain when Albert first appeared at the Habenhowe house on Pilcox Hill. Henry Mayfield always claimed to have been the first to see him when he made a call on his goddaughters one day in the middle of November. He described him as a rather good-looking, dark-haired young man. "Modern . . . well-dressed," he added, thinking of the well-cut suit and the smart shoes. Mayfield hadn't spoken to him, only noticed him talking to Hugh in the garden. "Who's that?" he'd asked when Georgette came to the gate. "That's Albert," she'd answered, "and it isn't convenient for you to call today." He'd left in some annoyance at her arrogance.

Some people said that Albert hadn't been in evidence before the twins went away for a week in mid-November leaving Hugh Cole with his mother and stepfather. So the girls must have picked him up then. He certainly wasn't local. But others maintained they had seen Albert around before then.

What was generally agreed was that the Habenhowe twins were behaving scandalously again. Robert Oakleigh's four-week sojourn with them had not passed unnoticed despite the isolation of Pilcox Cottage from the rest of the village. Now they had another man living there. The villagers shrugged. Well, it was only what you'd expect, they said. Remember what they were like at fifteen? Had practically every lad in Tanniford, didn't they? And everyone knew it was a bit queer them having that Hugh Cole up there in a caravan. Soft in the head he may be . . . doesn't mean there's anything wrong with his body. The tongues began to wag once more.

Dr Oakleigh heard the gossip. So too, did his wife. "Do you think I should say something in my next letter to Robert?" she asked.

"Certainly not," her husband said firmly. "This is typical village smut. We don't know what the truth is. I should say nothing until he comes down at Christmas."

Robert, however, came home before Christmas. He had become increasingly frustrated at the response to his letters to Georgette. Her reply to his first letter had been warm and friendly—although not as warm as he'd hoped and not as loving as his own letter. The next letter had been cool and impersonal and the last one he had received had been almost unfriendly. It was signed simply "G and G." At night in his room at college he was tormented by memories of those long, wonderful nights with her. He badly wanted to see her and to hold her in his arms again. On the spur of the moment he decided to cut lectures and go home to Tanniford on a long weekend.

When he arrived unexpectedly at his home, intending only to drop his bag and then to walk straight up to Pilcox Cottage to see Georgette, Dr Oakleigh intercepted him.

"You mean there's a man living there?" Robert asked incredulously as his father explained the situation. "I expect he's a friend of Georgina," he said without much confidence.

As Robert crunched along the lane to the gate of the house Hugh Cole poked his head out from the door of his caravan. He loped across the grass and by the time Robert reached the gate Hugh was standing the other side holding it closed.

"Don't be silly, Hughie, let me in. I've come to see Georgette."

"W-wait." Hugh threw back his head and whistled loudly.

The front door of the house opened and one of the twins looked out.

"Georgette?" Robert asked tentatively.

"No . . . Gina." She unhooked a coat from behind the door and walked down the path towards him pulling it on.

"I'd like to speak to Georgette, please."

Hugh moved aside as Georgina came to the gate. "Term doesn't end this early, does it?" she asked abruptly.

"No, I'm just down for the weekend. I'd like to speak to Georgette," he repeated.

"She's busy. She'll be out in a moment." She made no move to invite him into the house and the three of them stood in awkward silence, their breaths condensing in the cold winter air until Georgette emerged from the house and joined them. "Hullo, Robert, I thought you wern't coming home until Christmas."

"I wasn't, but I wanted to see you."

"Me? Oh . . . well here I am." Her tone was light as
though there had been nothing between them. As though
she hadn't spent all those nights in his arms quivering and
sighing with passion. He stared at her. Her violet eyes—
those eyes that so often invaded his dreams—were
neutral. Not cold like Georgina's, but not warm either.

"I'd like to speak to you *alone*," he said.

Georgina took Hugh by the arm and they moved away.
"Goodbye, Robert," she called over her shoulder. "Goodbye, Robert," Hugh repeated, parrot-fashion. Georgina
went into the house. Hugh returned to his caravan and sat
down on the steps outside.

"Well?" Georgette's eyes had softened slightly.

"What's wrong? What's the matter? Aren't you even
going to invite me in?"

She looked away from him. "I'm afraid it's not very
convenient at the moment."

"Is that why Hughie rushed to the gate like a bulldog?
Had his orders, had he?" Robert's tone was acid. He felt
deeply hurt.

"Hughie doesn't let anyone in unless they're expected,"
she said defensively.

"What about Albert?" He shot the name at her.

She dropped her eyes again. "Oh, you know about that."

"The whole village does."

"Yes, I suppose they would."

"Is he your friend or Georgina's?" It hurt his pride but he
had to ask. Her chin came up and she met his gaze steadily.
"Both of us, actually."

His eyes bored into hers. "He's more than a friend
though, isn't he?"

She averted her face. "Yes," she whispered.

The single word pierced him. If only she'd denied it. If
only she'd said he was Georgina's friend. Anything but
this stab to the heart.

"Who is he? Where does he come from?" he burst out
angrily.

"Please, Robert, it's nothing to do with you."

"Isn't it? Is he in there now?" He jerked his head towards

the house. "Why don't you introduce us? We could compare notes," he said through his teeth.

"Don't be so beastly!" she cried. "Oh, why are you being so horrible?"

"*Why*? Because I loved you. How could you do this? So soon after . . ." His voice broke.

"Don't be so upset," she pleaded. "It isn't fair." She sounded distressed.

"Not fair? Was it fair of you to let me love you night after night, letting me think—"

"That doesn't give you a hold over me," she said swiftly. He thought her choice of words was strange.

"I don't want a 'hold' over you, Georgette, as you put it. I just want to love you."

"You'll find someone else to love," she said gently. "Georgina says you will and you'll soon forget. She thinks—"

"Damn Georgina!" The pain and his wounded prided erupted into anger. "This is her doing, I'll bet." He ignored the warning flash in her eyes and plunged on recklessly. "You're *you*, Georgette. You're not the same as her. She'll wreck your life if you—"

He broke off. "Don't try to come between them," his father had warned. "Don't ever threaten their oneness." Well, he had. He'd done exactly that and he could read the result clearly in the sudden change in Georgette's expression. Her face stiffened. She didn't argue with him. She didn't defend Georgina. She simply said, "Goodbye, Robert," and turned on her heel. She walked up the path and into the house without looking back.

Robert left Tanniford again the same evening. "At least stay and have a meal before you go," his mother begged. "Thank you, I'm not hungry." She looked at his set face and didn't press the point. She aired her concern to her husband later. "He hasn't eaten a thing," she wailed.

"He won't die of starvation between here and his college," Dr Oakleigh said unsympathetically, turning the page of the paper he was reading.

"That wicked girl . . . she's broken his heart."

"A broken heart is not a medical condition," her husband said cheerfully. "Robert will live."

"Oh, how can you be so calm!" Janet Oakleigh exploded in exasperation. "I've never seen Robert so upset."

"I'm calm, my dear," said Dr Oakleigh, folding his paper and laying it aside, "because I happen to think that what has happened is for the best. There was no future for him with Georgette Habenhowe, no future at all. Neither she nor her sister is capable of a close, stable relationship with anyone. It's not their fault. They can't help themselves."

"I suppose you're right." His wife pursed her lips. "I wish he hadn't taken it so hard though. I don't understand him. It's not as though he hasn't had girls before."

"I imagine this was the first time he fell truly in love."

"But he only knew her for a few weeks in the summer."

"You forget, my dear. He has, in fact, known Georgette on and off for most of his life." He sighed. "Though I fancy those last weeks were rather special." He picked up his paper again. "Don't fuss. He'll get over it."

"I wish I felt as easy in my mind as you do," she said doubtfully.

The village continued to be aware of the twins' 'Fancy Man' as he came to be known because Georgina and Georgette seemed to make a point of flaunting Albert in front of them as though to underline their contempt for what people thought of them. Their two mopeds were frequently seen puttering noisily to the shops in the High Street with Albert mounted on one and either Georgina or Georgette on the other.

"It's disgusting, Henry!" Mrs Mayfield complained to her husband. "Two young girls having a man to live with them. You'd think they'd at least be discreet about it."

"Hughie has been there for a year and no one minded that," he said mildly.

"That's different!" Mrs Mayfield said tartly. "You know very well it is. Everyone knows Hughie and understands. Besides he doesn't live in the house. This man is obviously a *lover*." Marjorie Mayfield emphasised the word with obvious relish. "Before him they had Robert Oakleigh living there in the summer. Mrs Kronks told me so this morning. Can't you say something to them? After all, they're your goddaughters."

"No, I can't," he said firmly. "I'm not responsible for their morals."

"Then I shall speak to someone who is," she said. "I shall speak to the vicar."

The Reverend Gaye, as it happened, was willing to call on Georgina and Georgette—although not for the reason Mrs Mayfield gave him. The twins did not attend church and he hadn't spoken to them since their mother's funeral nearly two years ago. He had no intention of preaching the evils of fornication or of threatening them with Hellfire and Damnation as Mrs Mayfield would have liked him to. Past experience with the Habenhowe girls had taught him that it would have no effect. However, he did regard it as his duty to keep in touch with his flock and in the Reverend Gaye's eyes every person in the parish was one of his flock whether they attended church or not.

"Yes, I shall certainly call on them, Mrs Mayfield. It's high time I paid a visit. Thank you for reminding me."

If the vicar hoped also to see the newcomer to his parish when he visited Pilcox Cottage he was disappointed. Albert was not at home when he called—unless he was skulking upstairs, that is. Hugh Cole saw the Reverend Gaye striding along the lane in his black cassock and long before he reached the house had warned Georgina and Georgette of their approaching visitor. When the vicar reached the gate Hugh was already there holding it open for him on the twins' instructions. He greeted the black-frocked figure with his usual lop-sided, slightly vacant grin.

"Morning Hughie."

"Morning er . . ." But Hughie had lost track of the right word. The Reverend Gaye patted his arm reassuringly and marched on up the path to the front door.

It was some time after he arrived when Richard Gaye broached the subject of Albert. He had to admit that the two Miss Habenhowes had been quite friendly. They had even pinned on their name brooches for him so that he could address them correctly. And *most* hospitable. Well, it was a grey cold morning with a heavy frost on the ground and whisky was a sensible drink for such a day. Georgina had insisted. The whisky had been a very large one and then to his astonishment she had poured herself one every bit as large. He did hope she wasn't taking after her poor mother. Georgette, he was relieved to see, drank coffee.

"Is . . . um . . . Albert, I believe he's called . . . around? I thought I might introduce myself if he is." He peered at the two girls over the top of his spectacles. Georgina replenished his glass, ignoring his half-hearted protest.

"I'm afraid he's out," Georgette said. "He won't be back until late tonight."

"Albert isn't religious, vicar, you needn't waste your time on him." Georgina poured herself another drink. Oh dear, he thought, she *is* turning out like her mother.

"Perhaps I'll catch him another time," he said. "Will he be staying with you long, may I ask?"

"No, probably only a month or two," said Georgette.

The answer surprised him. He would have asked more questions—tactfully, of course—but Georgina forestalled him.

"People in Tanniford are very nosey, don't you think, vicar? I mean . . . what we do up here is *our* affair, don't you agree? The villagers should mind their own business, shouldn't they?"

"Er—yes, my dear. Yes. Though I'm sure it's only because they have your welfare at heart that they take such an interest." He avoided their sceptical eyes.

When he left, Hugh Cole appeared at his side like a jack-in-the-box and escorted him to the gate.

"How do you get along with the . . . ah . . ." The vicar strained after a suitable phrase. ". . . gentleman guest?"

"You what?" Hugh's mouth hung open and his face was blank.

The vicar sighed and tried again. Subtle words were lost on Hughie. He pointed to the house. "The *man*," he said. "The man—what's he like?"

"Oh . . . him." Hughie's face cleared. "Good," he growled. "Very good. *Likes* me." Oh well, that was something, the vicar supposed as he trudged away glowing pleasantly inside with whisky.

When the twins traded in their mopeds for a low-slung, fast sports car the village were soon aware of the change

because Georgina and Georgette roared down to the Black
Dog in it the next Sunday lunchtime.

Billy Staton paused in the middle of polishing a glass as
they entered the bar. Billy had been barman at the Dog for
a year and the twins hadn't come into the pub before nor,
so far as he knew, did they drink in any of the other pubs in
the village. Heads turned and there was a drop in conversation as the twins approached the bar. They made a
striking couple in their identical outfits—plain grey pullovers over grey, pleated skirts—with their shining
chestnut-coloured hair. They carried identical black hand-
bags and each girl wore the letters of her name hanging
from a gold chain round her neck. It annoyed Billy to see
them immediately become the centre of attention as they
moved confidently forward and the men at the bar made
way for them.

Two pairs of eyes fastened on him. "Hullo, Billy." It was
Georgina who spoke. "Didn't know you worked here."

He nodded curtly. "What'll it be?" Even their attrac-
tiveness irked him.

"Whisky for me . . . a glass of red wine for Georgette." It
angered him to have to wait upon them and pour their
drinks like a servant. Old hostilities flared into his
memory as he banged the drinks down on the counter.

Georgina opened her bag and tossed a twenty-pound
note in front of him.

"Is that the smallest you've got?" Billy snarled.

Her hand was halfway to her bag again when she looked
up and met the hatred in his eyes. She clicked the bag shut.
"Yes!" she snapped. "Why? Is your till empty or something?" Her voice had risen.

Billy, unable to argue in front of the other customers,
snatched up the note and rang the till. He threw the
change on the counter in a heap. Georgina looked at it for
some seconds without moving. Then she reached forward
and deliberately spread the money out on the counter,
separating the notes and the coins. With studied care she
slowly counted first the notes and then the coins. "It's
right," she announced loudly, manufacturing a tone of
surprise. Billy seethed. One or two onlookers tittered.
Georgina transferred the money to her handbag and she

and Georgette turned and carried their drinks to a table, ignoring the curious glances and the admiring looks.

Billy soothed himself with anticipatory thoughts of the afternoon meeting with Justin Mayfield. On Sundays, after he'd finished at the Black Dog and he'd had a belly-full of beer, he met up with Justin and they wandered around the shipyard together. Billy knew a door to one of the sheds that was always left unlocked. Billy looked forward to Sunday afternoons.

FIFTEEN

Henry Mayfield gazed sadly at his son. Justin's long eye-lashes fluttered nervously as he lowered his eyes and turned his face away from his father. "What incredibly beautiful eyes the boy has," Mayfield thought. He stared at Justin's bowed head, the dark curly hair, the soft outline of his face with its flawless complexion. The boy was *pretty*—there was no other word for it. A boy of sixteen had no business to look like that.

Mayfield felt ashamed at having searched his son's room while he was out. He had thought that Justin's association with Billy Staton had ended some time ago but it seemed he was meeting him secretly. Yesterday his wife had told him in a worried voice:

"Mrs Kronks thought we ought to know that her husband saw Justin and Billy Staton in the shipyard on Sunday. They were coming out of one of the sheds and Staton had his arms round Justin."

Mayfield decided to act. The search had been easy. Justin was obsessively tidy and his room was neat and clean. Not like his sister's. Estelle's room was like a rubbish tip. Mayfield was prepared for the female clothing in one of the cupboards although he was surprised at the quantity and variety of it. He'd seen some of Justin's performances both in school plays and in productions by the local amateur dramatic society. They were good and although he found the idea distasteful he was half-reconciled to his son making a career as a female impersonator.

He found the poems in a locked drawer. The key had been hidden in another drawer. Sheets and sheets of Justin's neat writing. As Mayfield scanned through them he was appalled. There was no mistaking the meaning of the poems or the depth of knowledge they revealed of matters that Mayfield preferred to close his mind to. He held them in his hands now as he stood over Justin wondering how to proceed.

"Don't you think you owe me an explanation?" he asked.

Justin's head reared up. "Me owe *you* an explanation?"

he cried. "You sneaked in here and pawed through everything! I'll never forgive you for that!"

"Don't take that line with me, boy!" his father blustered.
He thrust the sheets of paper into Justin's face. The pages
quivered as his hands trembled with the force of his
emotions. "These poems are filth!" he shouted. "Sheer
filth!"

"You *would* think that," Justin said bitterly. "You don't
understand them."

"Don't I?" his father challenged. "Their meaning is clear
enough to me, thank you. So is the person you've written
them to." His lipe curled. "*My darling Billy* . . . I'll bet he
loves that, doesn't he?"

"He hasn't seen them," Justin said sulkily.

"Oh." Henry Mayfield's spirits lifted for a moment.
Perhaps it was all in the mind. But then he remembered
the shipyard. "How involved *are* you with Bill Staton?"

"Involved? What do you mean, *involved*? He's my
friend."

"You know very well what I mean."

"No I don't, father. Tell me. Spell it out." Justin's eyes
were mocking and unnaturally bright.

With an effort Mayfield held on to his temper. "I don't
think your relationship with him is a good thing. I'd like
you to end it," he said quietly.

"No!" There was an edge of hysteria in the defiant voice.
"Billy is my friend. I won't allow you to choose my friends
for me."

"Son . . ." Mayfield put a hand on his shoulder.

"Don't touch me!" Justin jerked away violently. There
was loathing in his eyes. "I hate you! I hate you for prying
and poking about in my room. You won't break up Billy
and me. You can't stop me being friends with him."

"We'll see about that," Mayfield said grimly and turned
to leave.

"Give me back my poetry! It's mine!"

Mayfield hesitated, then threw the sheets of paper on
the bed and walked out of the room.

That evening as Billy Staton left the Black Dog after
closing up he found Mayfield waiting for him.

"I'd like a word with you, Staton."

"Oh yeh, what about?"

"My son."

Billy's eyes narrowed. "What about him?"

"We can't talk here." Mayfield looked up and down the street. Staton's home in Ferry Street was only a short distance away but Ruth might be there and that would be embarrassing. "Let's go down on the quay."

They walked down the short slope to the quayside and sat on one of the wooden seats there. The quay was deserted and silent except for the lap of water. Lights from nearby houses danced on the ebbing tide.

"I'd like you to stop seeing Justin." Mayfield had decided on a calm, reasonable approach. "He's an affectionate boy but he's mixed-up—emotionally, I mean. He seems to have a very strong attachment to you and . . . well, frankly, it's unhealthy."

"What makes you think that?" Billy asked cautiously.

"I found some poems in his room. Poems about you. They're very explicit."

"To me? Poems?" There was amused surprise in Billy's voice. "Well, well."

"Staton, Justin is only a boy. He's barely sixteen. You're a man. It's up to you to stop this."

"What does Justin say?"

"He refuses to end the association. That's why I'm asking you to."

Billy Staton relaxed. It was all right. Justin hadn't blabbed. He wanted to carry on, the little hot-ass.

"I like the lad. I don't see why I shouldn't be friends with him."

Mayfield's tone changed. "Very well, Staton, I'm not asking, I'm *insisting*. You will leave my son alone. Those poems may not be *proof* of anything but . . ." He let the implied threat hang in the air.

Staton's face became wolfish in the gloom. "You've got a nerve, threatening me, Mayfield, a bloody nerve! I remember what you got up to with young Ruthie when we used to come to your house on a Saturday."

Henry Mayfield was taken aback. "That was years ago," he muttered. "I don't know what you're talking about."

"Oh yes you do. You corrupted her, Mayfield. You

warped her mind. That's why she took up with Hughie."
His voice sharpened. "And now she's having it off with his
stepfather—Lionel Cole. Did you know that?" Henry
Mayfield shook his head, sick at heart. "*You* did that,
Mayfield. *You* taught her to like it with a man old enough
to be her grandfather."

"That's ridiculous! I didn't do anything. I . . ." His voice
faltered. Perhaps Ruth . . .? She always gave him such a
sweet smile when he saw her. Surely she wouldn't have
betrayed him?

Billy thrust his head forward. "Like me to jog Ruthie's
memory? Get her to have a chat with your Justin? She
couldn't half make his ears wiggle hearing about you, I'll
be bound, if I asked her to."

Mayfield glared at him in shock and horror. "You
bastard!" he said angrily. "You foul bastard!"

Billy stood up and stretched languidly. "You just keep
your nasty little thoughts 'bout me and Justin to yourself
. . . *councillor*. You are still a councillor, aren't you?" He
laughed unpleasantly as he walked away in the darkness.

Mayfield rose and moved to the edge of the quay. He
stood staring down into the restless water. Ruth and Cole?
She couldn't be much more than seventeen. Did Carol
know, he wondered. That's how young *she* had been
when . . . But then he'd been only twenty-seven himself,
not old and sour like Cole.

His thoughts returned to Justin. He hadn't been much of
a father to him. Nor to Estelle, come to that. He shuddered
as he thought of the harm Staton could do with his foul
mouth . . . guessing, exaggerating . . . making everything
sound worse than it had been. He kicked a stone into the
water. Something would have to be done about Billy
Staton.

Robert made several attempts to write to Georgette. He
was entitled to an explanation and she had offered him
none. There had to be a reason for their conduct—the
twins always had their reasons for what they did, no
matter how crazy these might sound to other people. But
he couldn't find the right words with which to ask. He
wouldn't plead and it was no use demanding. In the end

every letter he wrote ended in his waste-bin.

The Habenhowe twins visited the Black Dog again the next Sunday. Billy saw the two heads of short, coppery hair threading a way through the crowded bar and gritted his teeth. Why couldn't the bitches do their drinking somewhere else? Their very presence would spoil his Sunday morning. They wore the same grey outfits and necklets as last time and, as before, people stared curiously as they sauntered to the counter. Billy busied himself serving other customers and deliberately kept them waiting. At last he allowed Georgette, nearest the counter, to catch his eye. He gave her a big, false, smile.

"*So* sorry to have kept you waiting, ladies," he said with mock politeness. "What would you like?"

"A glass of red wine and a whisky," Georgette said tersely.

"The rate *he* serves you'd better make that a double, Georgie," snapped Georgina over her sister's shoulder.

Billy flushed with anger. Leaning towards Georgette he inclined his head at Georgina and said venomously:

"Taking after her old ma, is she? Can't get the booze down fast enough?" He stooped down below the counter, reaching for a glass.

Suddenly a freezing deluge engulfed his head. Georgette had picked up the jug of iced-water standing on the counter and emptied the entire contents over him. There was an immediate hush in the conversation in the bar.

She leaned forward over the bar-counter. "Don't ever insult my sister or our mother again, you creep," she said, white with fury.

The landlord, his ear carefully attuned to the sounds in the bar, had been snatching a quick lunch in his parlour. He came out to see what had caused the sudden quiet and stared at his barman rising up like a man from the sea, his wet hair dripping over his forehead.

"What's going on?" he demanded.

Georgette bent forward again. Her eyes were hard. "Tell him, Billy," she said softly, "and make sure you tell him *why*."

Billy reached for a cloth and began wiping his face. "It

was an accident," he mumbled. "I knocked the jug over as I bent down."

"Clumsy bugger," said the landlord. "Mop it up."

Billy Staton fumed with rage as he cleaned up and continued serving. His rage burned all morning, fuelled by the sight of Georgina and Georgette drinking and laughing in his bar until closing-time. Each time one or other came to the bar for more drinks his hands shook with suppressed anger as he served them. He swore he'd find a way to make Georgette sorry for what she'd done to him. He'd pay her out for making a spectacle of him in front of the customers. By Christ, he would!

It didn't take Billy long to devise his revenge. He settled on a plan he'd used before, although then it had been for a different purpose. The next time she came into his pub to drink—the very next time, he promised himself—he'd fix Georgette.

He had to wait until the following Sunday when the red, two-seater sports car swept once more into the car-park of the Black Dog. Albert was at the wheel with one of the twins beside him. Billy waited in suspense to see which girl it was as the couple entered the bar. It was early and the bar was almost empty. She was wearing a fur-trimmed black coat, buttoned at the neck, and a Cossack-style fur hat. Billy's hooded eyes anxiously watched her unfasten the coat and throw it open as she moved elgantly to a table and sat down. Golden letters nestled against the black woollen dress beneath. He sighed with satisfaction. It was Georgette. He dropped his eyes as she glanced across the room at him. His stomach knotted with hate. She was looking at him as though he was dirt.

He greeted Albert affably as he came to the counter. "Yes, sir, what'll it be?"

"Half of bitter and a glass of red wine, please."

Billy smiled with relief. It would have upset his plan if they had both drunk the same. He eyed the foppish young man with curiosity as he dispensed the drinks. Albert was no he-man. He wondered what there was about him that appealed to Georgette . . . or Georgina . . . or—he smiled sardonically—both of them if that was how things were. He'd heard the bar-talk, the smutty comments, the throaty chuckles. "D'you reckon they wear them necklaces in bed so he knows which one he's in bed with? Don't suppose he cares though—they'd both seem the same."

Albert had dark hair under the smart Norfolk cap and there was a small, toothbrush moustache on his upper lip. When he lifted the cap to settle it more firmly on his head Billy saw that the hair was straight and brushed back without a parting. His clothes were well-cut and expensive. For some reason Albert's eyes seemed to fill with amusement when he caught Billy looking at him.

Billy watched him carry the drinks to the table and sit down. Georgette smiled at him as she raised the wine to her lips and took a dainty sip. Billy fingered the envelope in his pocket and followed her movements with almost loving attention. Albert leaned forward and said something and Georgette threw back her head and laughed. "Laugh, you bitch," Billy breathed, " 'cos you won't be laughing soon. You'll be rolling on the floor blind drunk like your old ma used to be."

There was plenty of time. He'd let her get a few drinks inside her first. The powder in the envelope was the product of three of Billy's mother's sleeping pills. He had carefully cut open the capsules and extracted the powder. Barbiturate and alcohol. It was a mixture Billy had once administered to a girl who had been reluctant to perform the way he wanted her to. He'd slipped the powder into her gin and tonic the next time he took her out. Twenty minutes later she'd been staggering about, stoned out of her mind. By then Billy had steered her to the shipyard. There, slumped over a packing-case, she was soon made to accept his way of doing things. Afterwards she'd thought she'd been drunk.

It was when Albert came to the bar for a third round that Billy doctored the wine. He'd already dropped the powder into a glass out of sight below the counter as soon as he saw Albert rise from the table. When Albert reached him Billy was filling the glass from a wine bottle.

"Same again, sir! I thought so. There we are . . . a nice red wine for the lady."

Albert picked up the glass and to Billy's consternation took a sip.

"And for you, sir?" Billy asked quickly. "A bitter, wasn't it?"

Albert rolled the wine round his mouth and swallowed. He smacked his lips. "No, I'll have a glass of wine too, this time."

Fumblingly, Billy poured another glass. If he could somehow . . . But there was nothing he could do and a moment later the two glasses were on their way to the table. He bit his lip in vexation as Albert retained the doctored glass and set the other one in front of Georgette. His plan had gone wrong. He wouldn't have the pleasure of seeing Georgette reeling about, apparently drunk, disgracing herself. Still there might still be a spectacle when loverboy lost the use of his legs and couldn't stand. That would shame Georgette and make her look silly. Billy glanced at the clock. Another quarter of an hour should see the fun starting; and the bar was filling up nicely.

Then, minutes later, the plan went wrong even further. Albert and Georgette looked at their watches, finished their drinks and walked out. Billy sank his nails into the palms of his hands in frustration. He heard the powerful engine revving and the squeal of tyres as they drove off. He looked out of the window. Albert was driving.

SIXTEEN

The crash occurred on the unmade road which led past the Spreadeagle and out of Tanniford over the hill through which the railway tunnel ran. The road was not much used by vehicles and it was assumed afterwards that Albert and Georgette must have taken this route as a short cut because they were late for an appointment.

No one actually witnessed the accident although Wally Kronks thought he must have arrived on the scene very soon after it happened. Wally was cycling back to the shipyard after visiting one of his watermen who lived along that road and was laid up in bed with 'flu.

As Wally rounded the sharp bend on the crest of the hill where the road descended into Tanniford, he saw a car across the road in front of him. The bonnet was embedded in the grass bank at the side of the road. He jumped off his bike, laid it down and ran to the car. It was then, as he told the policeman, Ted Jordan, later, that he saw Albert in the distance, stumbling away across the fields. He shouted after him but either Albert didn't hear him or he took no notice.

The front of the car was stove in and steam was hissing from the crushed radiator. The windscreen was shattered and there were fragments of glass everywhere. Some yards away, over the bank, was Georgette. "Lying on her back just like she was asleep," Wally recounted afterwards to Sergeant Jordan, " 'cept her head was at a funny angle. I knew it was Georgette from her necklet." Wally was not unused to accidents in his line of work and from a brief examination he was fairly sure she was dead; but he retrieved his bike and cycled as fast as he could to the first house with a telephone and summoned an ambulance. Then he phoned Ted Jordan. After that he toiled up the hill again and waited by the wrecked car.

Ted Jordan arrived first, bumping and bouncing up the unmade road in his white police car. The county ambulance appeared some minutes later, tearing along the top road from the other direction. There was no hurry though. Wally had been right. Georgette was dead.

The ambulance men removed her body and the police-man began taking measurements and making a sketch in his notebook. Wally told him about Albert. "Funny, him running off like that," he said.

"He may be in shock," Ted suggested. "Shock affects people in all kinds of ways. He could be wandering around completely confused."

Wally's eyes swept the wrecked car and the deserted road. "I wonder how it happened."

Ted grunted. "Albert will be the one to tell us that," he said, closing his notebook. "Meantime, I'd best get up to Pilcox Hill and break the news to her sister."

"She'll take it hard," Wally said. "They were so close, those two. This'll tear her apart."

"It's a bad business," Ted agreed gloomily.

When he reached the house he waved to Hugh Cole as he approached the gate. "Is Georgina in?" he called. Hugh shook his head. "Best to make sure," the policeman said. "Knock on the door for me Hughie, will you?"

Hugh lumbered to the front door and banged the knocker. A moment later the door opened and one of the twins stood there. "Except," Sergeant Jordan thought sadly, "you couldn't say 'one of the twins' anymore." Georgina had lost more than a sister. That extraordinary likeness, that reflection of herself, had died too. The Habenhowe twins had ceased to exist. He had known them for almost as long as he'd been Tanniford's policeman— since he was a constable in fact, consoling their poor mother when the little devils had been reported to him for stealing sweets or fruit from the shops. They would never liven the village again. It was a sad, a very sad day he thought as he removed his hat and walked up the path.

"I'm afraid I have some bad news, Georgina."

"Yes?" Her eyes looked as though she'd been crying.

"Your sister has had an accident—a car accident. She's . . . I'm very sorry but I'm afraid she's dead."

She swayed on her feet but she didn't seem surprised. Ted Jordan had heard the tales about the Habenhowe twins—how they were supposed to have the same thoughts and to be able to feel each other's pains. Perhaps Georgina had already sensed her sister's death. Certainly her face had been tragic when she answered the door. She stared at him, eyes unseeing, without speaking.

At last she asked: "What happened?"

"There was a car crash—at the top of Rivenhall Road. It looks as though your sister was thrown through the windscreen and either the impact or the fall broke her neck. We won't know for certain until the post mortem." He heard her indrawn breath. "There will have to be a post mortem, of course."

"Yes," she whispered. Her eyes were wet with tears. "Poor Georgie."

"It seems the young man who's staying here was with her in the car. He wandered off though. Has he come back here?"

"No," she said decisively.

"Well, no doubt he'll turn up soon." He pulled out his notebook. "May I have his full name?"

She stared at him blankly. The policeman looked up, pencil poised. "His surname. We only know him as Albert."

"Jones," she said. "Albert Jones."

He wrote in his book and shut it. "When he returns ask him to contact me straight away would you, please?" She nodded. Sergeant Jordan put away his notebook and replaced his hat. "I'm afraid you'll have to formally identify your sister. I could run you to the mortuary now, if you feel up to it. It's best to get it over with," he advised. She nodded dumbly, her face crumpling.

At the mortuary Ted Jordan felt a wave of compassion as she looked at the cold, still face and said in a whisper: "Yes, that's my sister. That's Georgette." It was apparent that she was barely holding herself together, she was so overcome with grief.

That afternoon, when the sergeant returned to his house at the top of the High Street which served as the local police station, he confidently expected to hear from Albert Jones before the day was out. When he didn't do so he became puzzled. Not as puzzled as Billy Staton though.

The accident was the main topic of conversation in the Black Dog that evening. Billy listened to the speculations and theories flowing around him and none of them explained the point that bothered him. People were saying that Wally Kronks saw Albert staggering away across the fields although no one seemed to know whether or not he was injured. He wouldn't have gone far, Billy reckoned, not with three sleeping pills inside him—not for some time after, anyway. And yet he hadn't been found. So where the hell had he got to? That's what worried Billy. Was he badly injured—even dead, perhaps? Or was he lying low somewhere, wondering why he'd been so badly affected by a few drinks? Billy gnawed his lip with anxiety.

Sergeant Jordan was more formal on his next visit to Pilcox Cottage. He had made some enquiries, asked a few questions at the Black Dog and searched the area around the scene of the crash.

"We have to treat this man's disappearance very seriously, Miss Habenhowe. It is now evident that he was driving the car when he and your sister left the Black Dog and that he had been drinking immediately before the accident. The drinking may have nothing to do woth the accident, of course, but I have to tell you that the engineers have found no fault in the car's braking or steering mechanism and so far as we know no other vehicle or person was involved."

He was seated in the front room. Georgina was crouched forward in an armchair, shoulders slumped, only half listening to him. Her face was drawn and unhappy. Jordan's voice softened.

"It is most important that I speak to Mr Jones as soon as possible to clear this matter up. Are you sure you haven't seen him? He hasn't been in touch with you at all?"

"No," she answered dully.

"Isn't that rather strange . . . him not coming back here?"

"I suppose so." Her tone was apathetic.

"This man may have been the cause of your sister's death," the policeman said impatiently. "I should have thought you would be as anxious as anyone to contact him and find out what happened."

"What?" Her mind seemed elsewhere. "Oh . . . yes. What do you want me to do?"

"Well, can you suggest where he might be? Are there

any addresses among his belongings? Can you tell me more about him?"

Georgina's information about Albert filled less than four lines in Sergeant Jordan's notebook. There were no papers, no documents of any kind. She and her sister had met him in a seafront bar when they went away for a week in mid-November. The policeman had the impression that they'd picked the man up and had neither known nor cared who he was or where he came from. Apparently the village gossip about the Habenhowe twins and their morals was correct.

"Well, what did he *do*?" he asked in exasperation.

"Do?"

"Yes . . . *do*. Work. What did he do for a living?"

"Nothing." She met his eyes. "He didn't need to. We kept him."

The policeman dropped his own eyes. Ted Jordan was no prude. He dealt with too many of the sins of his fellow men to be that. But her frankness shocked him. Georgina had no helpful information about the man and the sergeant left Pilcox Cottage with no idea of where to begin looking for Albert Jones.

The post mortem wae carried out by Dr Oakleigh. Georgette had died of a broken neck and the cuts to her face were consistent with her having been thrown through the car windscreen. The autopsy was very thorough. In Dr Oakleigh's experience unexpected and quite irrelevant questions were sometimes put to the medical witness at an inquest. He did not intend to be short of information to meet even the most prurient question. However, the inquest was postponed until Mr Jones, whose evidence was vital, could be found. Meantime the coroner issued a burial certificate and the funeral took place a week after the accident.

"She may not have cried for her mother," The Reverend Gaye thought, as he stood at the head of the open grave and Georgina stooped and sprinkled a handful of soil on the lowered coffin, "but, my Goodness, she's weeping for her sister," He watched the tears flowing down Georgina's ravaged face and began composing some words of comfort to say to her.

He was given no opportunity to voice them, however, because after staring down at the coffin for a moment, Georgina let out a muffled sob and turned and ran blindly from the churchyard. Hugh Cole pushed his way through the small band of mourners and loped after her. She jumped into the waiting undertaker's car followed by Hugh and they were driven away.

Robert Oakleigh did not receive a letter from his mother telling him of Georgette's death until shortly before he came down from university for Christmas. Mrs Oakleigh had not wanted him to know until the whole business was over, believing this would be kinder. But the inquest had been postponed and the rumours had started and she'd had to tell him as he was now about to come home to Tanniford.

Robert wrote a brief note of condolence to Georgina, intending on his arrival in Tanniford to call and express his sympathy in person.

"She won't see you," his father told him. "She won't see anyone. The vicar has tried . . . Mr Mayfield has tried . . . and I've called myself. I did manage to spend a few minutes with her but she made it very plain that she does not want *anybody* to call, anybody at all."

"But she can't be left alone like that, it's too cruel!" Robert protested. "And Hughie won't be much help."

"I do rather side with Robert,". Mrs Oakleigh said. "It seems so un-Christian . . . especially at Christmas."

"Normally, my dear, I would agree wholeheartedly," said her husband. "But this girl is different. She has made it quite clear to me that she wants to deal with her grief in her own way and without help. She has to find herself again because, in a way, half of her has died too. You must leave her in peace for a while."

"O.K.," Robert agreed reluctantly, "if you really believe that's the right thing to do."

"I do."

"What about Albert Jones—has there been any news about him?"

"Not a whisper. He probably realises he could face a manslaughter charge and he's keeping well out of the way."

Robert said angrily: "You mean it was his fault Georgette was killed?"

"It could have been. He had been drinking and they say
the car had no mechanical defect. Of course, it might be
difficult to prove he was drunk since he wasn't breath-
alysed or blood-tested at the time. On the other hand there
may be a totally different explanation of the crash. But, if
so, it's hard to understand why he doesn't come forward
with it."

That Christmas was an unhappy one for a number of
people in Tanniford. Carol Cole awoke on Christmas
morning to find that her husband had not returned from a
Christmas Eve party the night before. Molly Staton, when
she eventually summoned the will to rise from her bed
that same morning, found a note from her daughter, Ruth,
saying that she'd run away with Lionel Cole. Lionel had
taken a job in a boat-building firm in the Shetlands, she
said, and she would live with him there until his wife
divorced him. The scandal of Ruth and Lionel running
away together spread quickly through the village and up
the hill to Mayfield Hall where it spoiled Henry Mayfield's
Christmas. Billy Staton, to everyone's surprise, was
subdued. Billy had other worries. He couldn't shake off the
haunting fear that Albert Jones was lurking somewhere,
cut and bloodstained, and biding his time to emerge and
accuse Billy of doping his drink and causing the death of
Georgette Habenhowe.

Hugh Cole, in his caravan, tore a lump of bread from a
loaf and plastered it with butter. He held the bread in one
hand and a wedge of cheese in the other and raised them to
his mouth alternately, taking great bites out of each with
his teeth and chewing steadily. Hugh could feed himself
simple fare like this but he was used to his meals being
cooked for him by the twins. He hadn't had a cooked meal
for some time, he reflected. Not since . . . Not since it
happened.

She herself hadn't eaten much either, he thought, and a
large tear rolled down his cheek. Hugh was lonely and
unhappy as well as hungry. Long ago, somebody had told
him that after you put people in the ground they went up
into the sky to where a place called Heaven or something

was. Everything was wonderful up there and everybody was happy. Even Hugh would be happy when he got there. You shouldn't cry for people who'd gone up there. But she cried all the time. She was crying now. He'd heard her when he crept to the window and listened.

Inside Pilcox Cottage the girl knelt on the floor, her eyes brimming with tears. Her hands were clasped together in an attitude of prayer. "Georgie . . . help me! If you can hear me . . . *tell me what to do*! They'll find out in the end. What shall I say?" She began rocking back and forth. "You *can't* be gone forever, I can't bear it," she wailed. "*I'm frightened*. I'm lost without you." She collapsed on the floor, sobbing.

SEVENTEEN

The New Year's Eve dance was held in Tanniford's village hall. It was not so much a dance as a jamboree—a kind of free-for-all—since the ages of those who came ranged from six to sixty. The annual jollification always ended with everyone, in the last quarter-hour before midnight, joining in the Conga. The long file of people—all hanging on grimly to the person in front—snaked out of the hall and into the street and sometimes in and out of the houses, before returning to the hall in time for the chimes of midnight.

The Mayfields arrived early so that Marjorie Mayfield could supervise her team of workers from the Women's Institute who were preparing the food. Henry Mayfield was press-ganged into the kitchen to help and left Justin and Estelle sitting in the hall looking bored.

Dolly Kronks also arrived early. Dolly meant to snap up a partner for the evening as quickly as possible and to hang on to him. There was always a scarcity of suitable partners because many of the younger men stayed in the pubs all evening, only showing up at the hall for the last dance. They'd come lurching into the hall in pullovers and jeans—jeans so tight you could see that they were thinking, her mother used to say—looking for a girl to walk home with. And they expected a good grope in some dark doorway on the way. Dolly wasn't having any of that tonight.

Her eyes lit up when Robert Oakleigh came into the hall. Now, *he* would do nicely. Dr Oakleigh's son would treat a girl with respect, she was sure, but she would wait a moment or two to see if he'd brought anyone. She cast her eyes round the hall, surveying the competition. That fat Estelle Mayfield had a hopeful look on her face *and* she was trying hard to catch Robert's eye. Without further hesitation Dolly hurried across the floor.

Robert gazed about him uncertainly. He hadn't really wanted to come to the dance but his mother had practically pushed him out of the house. "Go and meet some young people and have a good time," she'd insisted. "Don't sit around here with your father and me on New Year's Eve."

That afternoon he had stood by the mound of fresh earth in the churchyard for the second time. The flowers had been removed but one wreath remained. The card was limp with rain and the writing had blurred. He'd read it the first time. GEORGIE—DARLING SISTER. DEEPEST LOVE— GEORGIE. Robert still couldn't believe she was dead. It was some ghastly mistake.

"Hullo, Robert." He stared blankly at the girl in front of him, his mind elsewhere.

"You remember me. Dolly."

He returned to his surroundings. "Yes, of course. I'm sorry, I was miles away."

"Are you alone?" Dolly asked boldly, quite certain that he was.

"Yes, I am."

"So am I." She gave him the smile she'd been practising in front of her mirror and modestly lowered her eyes. Her fingers played with the smocking at the top of her off-the-shoulder dress, drawing attention to her nakedness. "You can't wear that dress," her mother had said. "You haven't the figure for it. You need to be fuller up top." Her hands described curves in the air. "Melons, not oranges." Dolly saw Robert's eyes appraising her bare shoulders and was glad she had stuck out against her mother.

Robert, however, was only thinking how thin she was. But Dolly was a cheerful girl and he felt badly in need of cheering up. He smiled at her. "Shall we team up then?"

"Oh yes, let's." Dolly breathed out. She had taken a deep breath to fill out the dress where it drooped slackly across her flat breasts. She linked her arm through Robert's possessively. Dolly had bagged her partner for the evening.

The Black Dog, along with the other pubs in Tanniford, had been granted an extension of licensed hours that night and Billy Staton had two extra barmen assisting him. Halfway through the evening he asked the landlord a favour. "Can I step out for a while round midnight? I'd like to be with me mum to see in the New Year. She's too ill to leave her bed and . . ." Billy put on a sorrowful face and allowed his voice to falter. ". . . and this'll probably be her last year."

The landlord regarded him sympathetically. Everyone knew that Molly Staton was going dotty. Ruth's elopement with Lionel Cole had just about sent her over the edge. "All right, Billy, but not more than half an hour, mind."

Billy had not the slightest intention of seeing the New Year in with his mother. As far as he was concerned she could rot in her bed. He hoped to have her put away soon. Her latest craziness should clinch matters. She'd started pegging sheets of toilet paper on the clothes line saying she was hanging out the washing.

Billy had an assignation with Justin Mayfield. "Sentimental little faggot," Billy had thought when Justin told him he wanted to share with him "those magic moments at midnight", as he called them. Billy's feelings were much cruder, on a different plane altogether. He expected to be well tanked-up with free drink by then. A quickie in the shipyard with Justin should round the Old Year off nicely. Billy indulged in lewd fantasies of synchronising himself with the twelve strokes of midnight.

There was a general exodus from the village hall when the interval came and people who wanted something stronger than coffee made for the pubs. Dolly and Robert joined those trailing down the High Street and over the railway bridge. The village hall was above the bridge, halfway up the hill almost next to Ted Jordan's house.

At the High Street entrance to the churchyard Dolly made to turn in, assuming they would follow the other people cutting through the churchyard to the Black Dog.

"No," Robert said abruptly, "not through there."

"But it's quicker and—"

"No. We'll go to the Anchor."

Dolly shrugged. She was disappointed. Her dad would be in the Dog and she would have liked to show herself off to him being escorted by Robert Oakleigh.

The Anchor, down on the quay, was packed solid. It was a mild night, with a moon, and after Robert had fought his way to the bar they took their drinks outside and sat on the quay.

Dolly sipped her gin and tonic. "Are you superstitious

about churchyards or something?"

"No. I just didn't want to go in there again. I've been there once today and it made me miserable."

Light suddenly dawned on Dolly. Her dad reckoned Robert Oakleigh had been sweet on one of the Habenhowe twins although he didn't know which one.

"Is it because of Georgette? Were you . . . fond of her?"

"Yes, very."

Dolly tried to find something helpful to say. "My dad found her, you know. He said she was lying on her back ever so peaceful . . . just like she was asleep." Dolly thought it might comfort him to know that.

"I doubt it." Robert's tone was harsh. "I know you're being kind but you forget . . . I'm a medical student. I've seen road accident victims. She would have been a mess."

"She *wasn't*." Dolly was slightly annoyed. "My dad wouldn't lie. She was neat and tidy and just as though she'd fallen asleep. Those were his words."

"Dolly, she was catapulted through the windscreen. She went flying through the air . . . almost certainly somersaulted . . . and landed on her head. How do you think *you'd* look?"

"Well, perhaps this Albert guy tidied her up before he ran off," Dolly suggested. "Maybe he didn't like to leave her all exposed and unladylike for everyone to see."

"Possibly," Robert muttered. He didn't want to dwell on the idea of Albert rearranging Georgette's body and her clothes after death. It reawakened thoughts of Albert and Georgette together.

"Dad saw him tottering away over the fields. I wonder where he went? Of course, you know what the old cows in the village are saying?"

"No, what?"

"They're saying he's hopped it because Georgina's got a bun in the oven and he put it there. And the reason she won't see anyone is because it's beginning to show."

"Damned old gossips," Robert said disgustedly.

They were silent for a while. Then Dolly giggled. "I've thought of another idea."

"What?"

"Maybe Georgina's murdered him. No, listen," Dolly

urged as he turned his head away from her. "Suppose Albert went back to Pilcox Cottage after the accident. It would be the natural thing to do. 'Georgina,' he says, 'I've just crashed the car and killed your sister.' What d'you think she'd do? You know how attached the twins were." Dolly's voice sharpened as she envisaged the scene. "She'd go mad! She'd kill him!"

Past memories of Georgina floated into Robert's mind. The way her eyes could harden and become implacable. Might she not indeed wreak a dreadful vengeance on a man who caused her sister's death? It was only too easy to imagine her, beside herself with grief and rage, seizing a kitchen knife and plunging it into the unfortunate Albert.

Robert said uneasily. "That's a terrible thought."

"Hey! I was only joking," Dolly told him with a laugh. "I don't *really* think Georgina would kill anyone, do you?"

"No, of course not." But he wasn't as sure as he sounded.

Down the slope from Pilcox Hill ambled the giant figure of Hugh Cole. He was bound for the shipyard on one of his weekly forays for kindling wood and logs for the solid-fuel stove in Pilcox Cottage. Regularly each week in the winter he took a large sack to the shipyard late at night and filled it with off-cuts of wood that had been left lying around by the carpenters and joiners who worked on fitting-out the ships. A bright moon shone from a cloudless sky and the countryside was as light as day. Hugh loved the moonlight. He cut across the fields to the top of Rivenhall Road and trudged down the unmade road and past the Spreadeagle. The doors of the pub were open and the radio was at full volume as the revellers in the bar monitored the approach of midnight. Hugh shook his head in bewilderment. Everyone was singing and laughing tonight. She'd been sobbing again when he left. He turned into the shipyard and began collecting wood and putting it in his sack.

In the village hall where the Conga was about to start Henry Mayfield suddenly realised that Justin was missing. He ran his eye methodically over the hall section by section and then checked the men's toilet. He went to the entrance doors.

"Have you seen my son?" he asked the man handling the

pass-out tickets.

"He slipped out about ten minutes ago, Mr Mayfield."

Henry Mayfield hurried out of the hall and down the High Street. He was pretty sure where the little fool had gone. Justin had pleaded to be left at home this evening, saying he didn't feel like going to a party. Mayfield had been convinced that it was merely an excuse to be free to see Staton and had insisted that Justin accompany the rest of the family to the party.

At the bottom of the High Street Mayfield turned left along South Street heading for the Black Dog. He would not endure this situation any longer. He'd had enough of fear. Ruth had left the village now. He would call Staton's bluff and threaten him with the police. He pushed open the door of the Black Dog, his eyes raking the faces of the men serving behind the bar. Staton was not there. Mayfield wasn't surprised. He knew where they'd be. In the shipyard. He turned towards Spring Street. By God, if he found the swine doing anything to the boy he'd . . .Henry Mayfield's fingers clenched and unclenched as he marched along.

Justin and Billy had met in the shadow beneath the stern of the vessel lying on stocks in the yard. The tide was high and the river was a glittering sheet of tiny lights as the moon was reflected in a thousand ripples. Justin thought the water was a beautiful sight. He started to explain his feelings to Billy.

Billy belched. "Yeh, yeh, it's lovely," he said impatiently. "Come on, I haven't much time." He took hold of Justin.

"You're drunk!" Justin said in disgust, pushing his hands away. "Stinking drunk."

"So what?" Billy took hold again.

"No! I didn't come here for that. No!" he shouted as Billy's grip hardened.

Billy's mood became ugly. "Don't you say no to me, you little faggot!" He forced Justin to the ground, pinning him face down over a baulk of timber. Over the night air came the distant chant of "I-Yi-Conga . . . I-Yi-Conga," as the singers jogged their way back into the village hall. "Hold still," Billy rasped. "You know you love it."

Inside the hall a worried Marjorie Mayfield took
Estelle's hand as the merrymakers formed a circle in
readiness for Auld Lang Syne and the end of the Old Year.
There was no sign of her husband and son. Dolly squeezed
Robert's hand and speculated on whether or not he would
kiss her when everyone shouted "Happy New Year!" If he
didn't, she decided, *she* would kiss him.

Hugh Cole had finished filling his sack with wood and
was leaving the yard when he heard the noises of a
struggle and then a boy's voice pleading. He padded
towards the sounds. When he came across Billy Staton and
Justin on the ground he didn't understand what was going
on but he realised that, whatever it was, the boy whim-
pering and wriggling beneath Billy didn't like it. A
massive hand reached down, grasped Billy by the collar
and hauled him off. Justin scrambled to his feet, adjusted
his clothes and stumbled away. Billy, choking and
cursing, broke free from Hugh's grip. He swayed about,
focusing hie eyes until he recognised his assailant. Swearing savagely, he picked up a length of heavy timber.
Wielding it like a club, enraged and reckless with alcohol,
he advanced on Hugh.

"I'm gonna smash your head in, looney!" he snarled. "I'll
brain you!" He raised the length of wood in a double-
handed grip, ready to deliver a crushing blow to Hugh's
head. Hugh stretched out his long arms. He clamped one
hand on Billy's shoulder and with the other took hold of
the piece of timber and pulled it effortlessly from Billy's
grasp and tossed it aside. He stepped forward, seized Billy
round the middle and lifted him into the air like a baby. He
looked about him, wondering what to do with his troublesome burden.

Henry Mayfield, approaching from the direction of the
bow of the ship, missed seeing Justin who had ducked
between the stocks supporting the vessel and was now
running back along the quay. Mayfield heard Billy's wild
threat and quickened his pace. Then, in the clear moonlight, he saw Hugh holding Billy above his head. He
halted. Hugh looked around for a moment and then
dumped Billy head first into an empty polythene bin used
for rubbish and wood-shavings. Hugh picked up his sack,

slung it over his shoulder and plodded off.

Billy's arms were pinned to his sides and his shoulders were wedged in the bin where it narrowed at the bottom. He began kicking, his legs bicycling the air. The movement, and his weight, overbalanced the bin. Mayfield watched it rolling to and fro near the top of the concrete launching slope. He expected Billy to crawl out backwards. Billy was firmly wedged, however. The bin slowly, very slowly, completed a revolution in one direction which brought it on to the launching way.

Mayfield told himself afterwards that there was nothing he could have done. That he was too far away. Yet he sometimes wondered whether, if he hadn't hesitated— debating what would happen—he could have acted in time.

The bin rolled over again ... then again. Mayfield started running. The bin gathered momentum and rolled faster and faster down the slope until it hit the water and floated off. Mayfield stopped halfway down the slipway and watched in helpless fascination as the bin began to fill with water, righting itself when it was half full, with Billy upside down inside. The bin was in mid-river now, moving fast on the ebbing tide. Billy's legs thrashed frantically as the water inside the bin covered his face and be began drowning. Thirty seconds later his legs jack-knifed and he was dead.

From the Spreadeagle behind Mayfield there were cheers and shouts as the first stroke of midnight boomed out on the bar radio, heralding the start of the New Year. In the village hall Dolly threw her arms round Robert's neck and kissed him hungrily.

The polythene bin bobbed past the mouth of the creek which the Habenhowe twins had so often painted in their pictures. There it filled completely, turned on its side and at last relaxed its deadly hold on Billy's pinioned arms and shoulders. The bin sank to the bottom of the river. Billy's body drifted on towards the sea.

EIGHTEEN

A few hours into the New Year, in the middle of the morning on New Year's Day, Dr Oakleigh was called to Pilcox Cottage. Hugh Cole came down on his bike bearing a note for him.

Earlier the same morning, a man walking his dog along the riverbank near the mouth found Billy Staton's body face down in the mud.

Robert Oakleigh awoke late. For a while the previous evening, he'd overcome his gloom. Dolly Kronks's bright cheerfulness had been a tonic. The depression returned because of something more she had told him. As they walked home after the dance she had been chattering about her friend Ruth Staton and Lionel Cole.

"How *could* she?" Dolly had shaken her head in bewilderment. "He's *middle-aged*. I'd curl up if someone like him touched me." After a moment she had gone on: "I don't know if I should tell you this, but Ruthie reckoned her brother Billy knew more than he's let on about that car accident."

"In what way?" Robert asked.

"Billy hated the Habenhowe girls, you know, really hated them."

"That was years ago though, when we were kids."

"No, recently as well. Billy insulted them or something and apparently Georgette tipped a jug of water over him in the pub in front of everyone. Billy was livid. Then, after the accident happened Billy was worried sick, Ruth says. And he was in a state about Albert—even went looking for him in the fields that night, she said."

"Why on earth would he do that?"

"Queer, isn't it? Ruth had the idea that Billy had fixed their drinks as a way of getting his own back and that he was afraid it would be found out and he'd be blamed for the accident. But surely they'd discover if Georgette had been doped or anything like that when they examined her, wouldn't they?"

"Not necessarily," Robert said. "It probably wouldn't show up if the autopsy was done more than twenty-four hours later."

"Ruthie must have had a reason for thinking what she did," Dolly mused. "She didn't explain though." A few steps further on she said: "Maybe that's why she ran off with old Lionel. She kept telling me she couldn't stand it at home much longer. Her poor ma is going batty and she was frightened of her brother." Dolly nodded her head in satisfaction. "That'll be why she did it." This was a more acceptable explanation to Dolly than that her friend could actually be enamoured of a man like Cole.

Later, in the passageway between Dolly's house and the rear of the scout hut, Robert kissed her goodnight. Dolly was eagerly amorous but her warmth had reminded him of how much Georgette had meant to him and his response had been half-hearted. Dolly seemed not to notice however, as she cooed and sighed contentedly. When they parted she told Robert that it had been her happiest New Year's Eve ever.

When Mrs Staton reported her son missing early on New Year's Day Sergeant Jordan didn't regard the matter too seriously until he checked with the landlord of the Black Dog and learned that Billy had not been seen after supposedly going home to his mother just before midnight. The landlord was furious that he hadn't returned to help with the clearing-up in the pub. After that it had not taken long for the body that had been found in the estuary to be identified as Billy's by an hysterical Molly Staton.

It was the first piece of news given by Dr Oakleigh when he returned to his house that morning and met Robert in the hall about to go out.

"Ted Jordan stopped me on the way back from Pilcox Cottage," he said. "Staton has been drowned apparently. I have another post mortem to do."

Robert, who had been hoping to call on Billy and force some information out of him about Georgette, felt frustrated rather than sorry. Then the rest of his father's words registered.

"Pilcox Cottage? You've been to see Georgina?"

"Yes. Hughie brought a note asking me to call." Dr Oakleigh laid down his bad and removed his overcoat.

"How is Georgina?"

Dr Oakleigh grunted. No point in making a secret of it. Everyone in the village would know soon. "Pregnant," he said bluntly.

Robert gave a resigned sigh. "So it was true after all," he said gloomily.

"What was true?"

"The village gossips had her pregnant by that fellow Albert."

"Well, it will be the first time they've been right about anything," Dr Oakleigh said tartly.

"Is that why Georgina sent for you—because she suspected she was pregnant?"

"No. She knew that already. It seems she had it confirmed weeks ago by some doctor on the other side of the county. No, she's suffering from the usual trouble . . . nausea . . . and rather badly. I've prescribed antihistamine and sent Hughie off to the chemist for her. Let's hope a baby will take her mind off her sister and give her an interest to look forward to."

Robert was busy with another train of though connected with what Dolly had told him last night. He began, "Dad, when you did the post mortem on Georgette . . ." No, he shouldn't ask about drugs in her body. His father was a stickler for medical ethics. He'd bawl him out for even asking. "Nothing," he said.

Dr Oakleigh, observing Robert's concerned expression, believed he knew the question his son wanted to ask. Had Georgette been pregnant too? Robert was torturing himself with thoughts of Albert and Georgette. He saw no harm in putting his son's mind at rest. "No, Robert, Georgette was not pregnant. In fact," Dr Oakleigh chose an old-fashioned way of putting it, "she'd been a good girl, had your Georgette." Robert stared at him blankly. Damn it, the boy was being a bit slow. "She was *virgo intacta*," Dr Oakleigh said crisply. "She'd never been touched." He was puzzled by the extraordinary expressions chasing across his son's face. Disbelief, amazement, shock, they were all there in succession. What was the matter with the boy? Wasn't he glad to know that?

Robert's mind was in a turmoil. It was not—*could not*

be—Georgette, the girl he'd made love to night after night, lying buried in the churchyard. *It had to be Georgina.* If his brain hadn't been so busy, jumping over itself, racing ahead, he would have blurted out the truth to his father. He'd have shouted with joy: She's alive! Georgette's alive! An hour later he was glad, very glad indeed, that he had remained silent. He took his duffel coat from its peg.

"Where are you going?" his father asked.

"To call on Georgina. I think she'll see me now."

Dr Oakleigh stroked his chin reflectively. "Yes, all right. But if your visit distresses her you're to leave at once, you understand? I don't want my patient upset."

"I'll be careful," Robert promised.

His mind was still in confusion as he hurried up the hill. Had they been playing their oldest prank—taking each other's place? Presumably the girl in the car with Albert had been Georgina pretending to be Georgette. But why keep up the pretence? Why carry it to such lengths? All kinds of wild thoughts went through Robert's head as he walked. The one shining fact he hung on to was that Georgette was not under that mound of cold earth in Tanniford churchyard. She was *alive*. Up there in Pilcox Cottage, God knows in what sort of crazy situation, but alive.

He slowed his pace as he realised that he had no knowledge of the mental state she might be in. His father had made no mention of her being distressed or disturbed during his visit but it would be unwise to suddenly confront her with his knowledge of her deception. For all he knew she *believed* she was Georgina. The shock of her sister's death might have turned her brain. He was certain she needed help desperately. He loved her and he wanted to help in any way he could; but the situation would need careful handling.

There was no sign of Hugh Cole as he approached the gate. Robert assumed he was still at the chemist's obtaining the prescription. He walked up the path to the front door and knocked softly.

"Who's there?" she called. "Is that you, Hughie?"

"No, it's Robert. Robert Oakleigh." He turned the handle of the door and it opened. He stepped through the

that he hadn't the heart.

She went on: "You see, we chose you because you seemed intelligent. Also, so far as we could make out, you had a healthy family background." She lowered her eyes. "And I liked you . . . a lot. That sort of settled it." She raised her eyes again and said earnestly: "We gave the matter a great deal of thought, you know." She seemed anxious to assure him of that.

"Georgette, I haven't the faintest idea what you're talking about."

"It's quite simple," she said. "Gina and I wanted a child."

He goggled at her as she continued in a matter-of-fact tone, "Marriage was out of the question. Neither of us would ever have left the other and we couldn't have shared our lives with a third person. We planned it all very carefully. The first part—once we'd decided on you—was easy." She gave him a coy look. "I had no idea it would be so nice. Gina was amazed too."

"But I didn't—"

"Robert Oakleigh, will you please keep quiet until I've finished this part," she said severely. "It's difficult and embarrassing and I have to explain it in my own way." She lowered her head and said quietly: "Yes, you were very sweet and concerned and you took a lot of trouble *not* to make me pregnant. I had a tricky time persuading you that you didn't need to bother."

He remembered. He could remember every moment of those wonderful weeks and the gloriously happy nights. Very early on she'd told him she was on the Pill.

"You must take it for two weeks to be sure you're safe," he'd warned her. He hadn't been so besotted as to forget his medical training.

She had nibbled his ear and murmured, "Yes, I know. And the two weeks are up, darling."

He'd lifted his face away from hers on the pillow. "But that would mean you started before we—"

"Yes. Aren't I wicked?" She'd buried her face in his neck and giggled.

Still he'd prevaricated. "But you couldn't have known in advance that I was going to make love to you."

"I knew you *wanted* to. Same thing," she'd said laughing. He'd believed her and from then on he'd taken no precautions himself when they made love.

He was stunned. Something their mother had once said came back to him. "You wouldn't believe the tricks those two can get up to," she'd told him. He stared at Georgette, not sure whether he wanted to laugh or to cry. She was looking down at the floor, digging at the carpet with the toe of her slipper.

He said stupidly, "So, the baby you're carrying is mine?"

She raised her head. "No, not yours, *mine*," she said. "You're the father."

He let the distinction pass. "Why didn't you tell me? I *loved* you. We could have married and—"

"Robert, the last thing we wanted to do was to wreck your career and saddle you with fatherhood. Besides, as I've already explained," she said patiently, "we wanted the baby for ourselves. I could never have left Gina. We were one . . . the same person. It was unthinkable that we'd separate. You knew us better than anyone so you, of all people, should understand that."

"I suppose I do," he agreed reluctantly. "But did you have to treat me the way you did? It was a pretty rotten way of breaking things off."

Her head drooped again. "I know. It was horrid. I hated that part. We honestly didn't expect you to mind so much. We didn't understand properly or imagine you falling in love with me. Georgie said you'd be all right after a time and anyhow there was no other way of making our plan work."

"You could have let me down more gently . . . taken longer to cool me off as it were," he said sourly, "before you leapt into another man's arms."

"No we couldn't. As soon as we were sure . . . sure that . . ." Her voice faltered.

"Sure that I was a satisfactory stud, you mean," he said harshly. "That I'd done my stuff."

She raised her eyes and studied him. "You're still hurt, aren't you?"

"Yes, I am," he admitted.

"But you see we *had* to bring Albert in quickly," she said, "so that when I began to show, everyone would think he'd been my lover and that the child was his. We only needed him around for about three months and the plan would have been complete." She went on dreamily: "It was a lovely plan. We were going to have such fun bringing up the baby, Georgie and me." She stared into the distance and her eyes moistened. "And now it's all gone wrong," she said sadly. She had the voice of a little girl whose doll has been broken.

Robert stood up and went to the window wondering if Hugh would return soon. "What about Albert?" he asked. "What happens when he shows up again?"

"Oh, he won't come back," she said confidently.

A tremor of alarm went through him. If he believed Georgina capable of killing Albert he had to accept that if the positions were reversed Georgette would be equally capable. He gazed out on to the garden trying to imagine the scene. The man staggering back here, half-drunk perhaps, admitting he'd crashed the car and killed Georgina. Robert could see it all. Georgette . . . he shuddered. Hugh Cole . . . digging. Hugh would do anything she asked. He turned round from the window. He had to know.

The room was empty.

NINETEEN

For a minute or two Robert had the illusion that he was living a dream, that he'd imagined his conversation with Georgette and that she wasn't here in the house at all. Then reality reasserted itself. She would return in a moment.

He turned and stared out of the window again. He had often sat at this window in the summer revising his notes while the twins worked quietly at their embroideries. He recalled the happiness and contentment . . . the sense of being in a different world from his own. He was in a strange world again now but this time it was chaotic, not the peaceful place he'd known when he was here before. His feelings were in disarray, his thoughts disjointed and he'd never been so unsure of his emotions as he was at present. He made an effort to discipline his mind and to organise his thoughts. He had three realities to cope with now. Three rocks amid the swirling waters. Georgette was alive. Georgette was pregnant. He, Robert, was a father-to-be.

There was a movement on the stairs behind him. Robert whirled round. The dull January day that lit the room barely reached the foot of the stairs where a figure stood in the gloom. Robert knew who it was however, in the Norfolk cap and the smart sports clothes. The man fitted perfectly the descriptions he had heard. "A natty dresser," his mother had said. "Dandy," was the word his father used. "Rather dashing and quite nice-looking," That had been Dolly Kronks's opinion. So, Albert Jones had been here in hiding all the time.

Robert remembered his manners. He stepped forward and extended his hand. "How do you do? I'm Robert Oakleigh." The hand he grasped was soft. But it was the suppressed giggle that broke the spell. He held on to the hand and pulled the figure forward into the room and into the daylight. The giggle turned to laughter as she tore off the cap and released her piled-up chestnut hair. "How do you do? I'm Robert Oakleigh," she mimicked, and burst into fresh laughter. She peeled off the false moustache.

"It's impossible!" Robert said foolishly, his mouth hanging open. "I can't believe it."

"I couldn't manage the wig—it takes ages to fit properly—and the trousers won't fasten over my fat tummy. But I wasn't bad, was I? I fooled you."

"Yes you did, for a moment. So *you* were Albert then? *You* were driving the car?"

She stopped laughing and gazed at him in astonishment. "Me? No. It was Gina. She was much better at Albert than I was. She was terrific. She could put on a deep voice and imitate a man's walk. We had a great time going round the village and in and out of the shops. And the pub . . . the Black Dog . . ." She began laughing again. "That was fantastic! Billy was a scream. He kept calling her 'sir'."

"But if Gina was . . ." Robert shook his head helplessly. "I still don't follow. Tell me about the accident."

Her face sobered. "That was terrible." She moved to an armchair and sat down. "We suddenly decided to drive to the beach. I didn't realise Georgie had had so much to drink. At the top of the hill—after we'd left the pub—she began swaying forward over the wheel. I thought she was fainting. I tried to move her aside. Her seat-belt must have come undone . . ." Her voice broke in a sob. "When we struck, she was thrown out through the windscreen. I was still in my seat, not hurt at all. I jumped out and ran to her. She wasn't breathing. I listened for her heart. Then I felt her pulse. I couldn't believe it." Georgette put her face in her hands. "She was dead. It was awful," she whispered, "as though the life had gone out of me too."

She stopped speaking and stared at the floor. Robert sat down in a chair and waited for her to continue. After a while Georgette lifted her head. "I couldn't let her be found like that—disguised as Albert. Everyone would have sniggered and laughed at us and our lovely scheme would have been ruined. I knew what she would have done in my place and I did it. I changed clothes with her. There was no one about. She was wearing her own underclothes and it only took a few moments. Then I smashed the windscreen a bit more so that it would look as though I had gone through it too. I didn't try to put on the wig and moustache because I saw someone coming along on a bike. I ran home over the fields, slipped in the back door without Hughie seeing me and changed into my own clothes again."

Robert felt the tension leaving him. The whole story was clear at last—even the reason for the dead girl's clothes being so tidy and why she had seemed to be drunk. No point in distressing Georgette with the truth about that last point, though. Billy was dead now.

Georgette stretched her arms above her head. "I do feel better. It's been such a relief telling you." She put her arms down and looked at him. "I'm in a dreadful mess, aren't I? That wretched Sergeant Jordan is still looking for Albert. Gina has been buried as me. I've told lies all round. And I'm going to have a baby." She smiled weakly. "I'm in rather a lot of trouble, aren't I?"

He nodded, preoccupied with the solution. His brain was in gear again, functioning normally after the confusions and doubts.

"Well, *help* me," she said impatiently. "That's what you're here for. You said to trust you. I do. I'll do anything you say."

She was incredible . . . amazing . . . outrageous. Various descriptions flitted through Robert's head. But he loved her. He loved her very much indeed. He started to smile.

"Don't sit there grinning," she said. "Tell me what to do."

"Would you marry me, Georgette?"

"Yes, of course I would now," she said impatiently. "But that won't help. I'll probably be sent to prison for what I've done."

"No you won't. Marry me and leave your story exactly as it is," Robert said, "and no one will ever be able to prove it wrong."

She turned her head slowly and stared at him. "You mean . . . say *nothing*? You'd marry me as Georgina? Let everyone—your parents . . . everybody—go on thinking I'm carrying Albert's child?"

"Yes."

"You'd do that?" she asked wonderingly. "For me?"

"I love you."

"I don't see how you can. I've deceived you . . . tricked

you . . . and I hurt you badly."

"Love doesn't end because someone hurts you."

"I think mine would," she said doubtfully.

He rose from his chair and went to her. As he bent and took her hands she looked up at him, her eyes vulnerable and appealing. "I'm frightened, Robert."

He pulled her gently to her feet. "There is nothing to be frightened of, my dearest. Trust me. Everything will be all right." He took her face in his hands and kissed her. She was unyielding at first. Then all at once she threw restraint aside and began returning his kisses passionately. Her arms went round his middle and she clung to him tightly so that he could feel the swelling in her abdomen as it pressed into him. In a pause for breath she raised her face and said: "You're a very nice person, Robert Oakleigh. I think I shall fall in love with you soon—" Her eyes widened and her voice changed. "Like right now," she said urgently.

He lifted her in his arms. She began kicking off the trousers as he carried her upstairs.

She was a wild creature in bed, wanton and abandoned. Robert was swept along by her passion to a new paradise even more wonderful than the one he'd entered with her before.

When the heat and excitement had gone out of them and they were calm again, she lay beside him tracing patterns on his bare chest with her fingers. "You know what they'll say in the village?"

"What?"

"They'll say I've bewitched you."

He smiled at her lovingly. "Well, you have, haven't you?"

She kissed his chest. "Yes. You're a Nurd now."

"What's a Nurd?" He stroked her hair.

"A Nurd is someone very special," she explained solemnly. "Someone I love and who loves me. There were only three Nurds in the whole world. Georgie, me and Hughie."

"What were the rest of us then?"

"Ords—except for the really horrible ones like Billy Staton. He's a Sloud."

They lay quietly together, relaxed and content.

"There might be another Nurd soon," Robert said after a while.

She frowned. "I don't think that would be possible."

"You're forgetting someone." He patted her stomach.

She looked down and turned on her back. Her middle began to wobble like a jelly as she shook with laughter. "You're right. There's a Nurd in there. L-look," she gurgled, "it's moving."

Robert lifted his head and watched for a moment, then collapsed helplessly beside her.

Pilcox Cottage rang with their laughter.

Billy Staton's funeral was held eight days into the New Year. They buried him next to the grave now marked by a headstone carved with the name: GEORGETTE HABEN-HOWE. No one—no one, that is, excluding Henry Mayfield but including the coroner—had any doubts about how Billy had met his death. Fuddled and filled to the brim with drink, he had staggered out into the night and fallen in the river. That's all there was to it. The only point of dispute—and it was merely an academic argument between the watermen and the welders in the shipyard—was about the exact spot at which Billy had gone into the water.

The welders plumped for the jetty at the bottom of Ferry Hill, just down from the Black Dog; but the watermen said scathingly that welders knew nothing of tides and drift and that if he'd gone in there he would have quickly washed up in the shipyard. They favoured a position on the riverbank down river from the yard. But of course, as they pointed out, it all depended on Billy's weight and his buoyancy factor and to illustrate the problem many a diagram was traced with a beer-laden finger on the bar counters of the Spreadeagle and the Black Dog. Billy would have been astonished at how much interest his drowning aroused.

There were not many people at the funeral. Ruth Staton came down from the Shetlands—without Lionel Cole—and collected her mother from the hospital where she'd become a voluntary in-patient the day after she'd had to identify her son's body. Ruth was apprehensive when she saw Carol Cole among the mourners and regarded her timidly as she came up to her after the service.

"There's no call to look at me like that, my girl," Carol said, drawing her aside. "I'll not add to your sorrow this day by quarrelling with you. I want you to carry a message for me . . . to *him*."

"Yes, Mrs Cole," Ruth agreed nervously.

"Tell him I'm bringing Hughie back home with me where he belongs. And I don't want to see his miserable face ever again," Carol said. "That goes for you too, miss. You've made your bed—now you lie on it. And stay away from Tanniford, the both of you." She turned on her heel and walked away.

Robert and Georgette were married at Tanniford church a month later. Len Stewart was the best man and Estelle Mayfield was bridesmaid. During the service the Reverend Gaye kept his eyes firmly on the couple's faces and his prayer book lest they should stray to the fullness of the bride's wedding-gown. He'd been forewarned when they came to him to put up the banns. "I wouldn't want you to be taken by surprise, vicar," she had said.

Brides with bulges beneath their bridal dresses were nothing new to Richard Gaye but he was astonished that Georgina Habenhowe should be one of them and even more astonished that Robert Oakleigh should be marrying her. However, he had rarely seen a couple who looked so happy and so in love. That was a blessing at least, he thought.

Len Stewart, also, was surprised at Robert's sudden union with Georgina. He wondered what he could have missed in her that evening when the four of them had gone to the beach and eaten fish and chips.

The bride was given away by her godfather, Henry Mayfield. Like the vicar, he too was privy to the situation but he had kept it from Mrs Mayfield. She would not have allowed their daughter to be bridesmaid if she'd known. On the day of the wedding he braced himself for the moment when his hawk-eyed wife would discern the truth of the village gossip. The moment came when the photographs were being taken in the churchyard after the service. A sudden gust of wind wrappled the loose gown tightly around the bride for an instant as she posed with her husband.

Henry Mayfield could almost hear his wife's eyes pop. Her grip on his arm closed like a vice. "She's *pregnant!*" she hissed in his ear.

He savoured his moment of triumph. "Yes dear, I know."

"You *knew*?" She was incensed.

"Yes. She thought it only fair to tell me as I was giving her away. She asked me to keep it a secret." The last part was untrue but it made an ideal excuse for not having told his wife.

"Well, it can't be his," Marjorie said smugly. "It must be that Albert Jones man's. What ever is Robert thinking of?"

Robert's mother had put the same question to her husband after Robert had told them of his intended marriage.

"*Georgina*? What ever is Robert thinking of?"

"I know, my dear," Dr Oakleigh said sympathetically. "I don't understand it either. But you must admit they both seem ecstatically happy. I've never seen Robert looking so happy. And I must say that girl has made a remarkable recovery."

"But she's going to have a baby!" Mrs Oakleigh wailed. "And it's not his. Oh, he's a *fool!*"

Dr Oakleigh poured himself a large brandy—something he seldom did in the middle of the day. "I don't think so. Robert isn't a fool. Nor is he a saint." He warmed the brandy-glass in his hands. "The way I see it is this. When he stayed with them last summer they must have played a trick on him. You know what they were with their tricks. He thought he was with Georgette but actually he was squiring Georgina."

"Squiring? It's a long time since I heard that word. What does it mean?"

"He went to bed with her," Dr Oakleigh said baldly.

"Oh, I see." Mrs Oakleigh adjusted her thoughts. "What about Mr Jones then?"

"I imagine he was Georgette's boyfriend and, incidentally, the gossip about her was wrong as usual. She wasn't promiscuous at all. But I should think he's gone for good now. There will be a verdict of 'misadventure' at the inquest and that will be the end of that."

"So you think the child *is* Robert's?" his wife asked in a hopeful tone of voice.

"I can't make sense of things any other way."

"Then why doesn't he tell us?"

Dr Oakleigh shrugged. "I don't know. I expect he will one day."

"There's his career to think of too. Will he go on with it? I did so look forward to him becoming a doctor like you, dear."

"And so he will," Dr Oakleigh said cheerfully. "Robert told me he has every intention of qualifying next year." He took a mouthful of brandy and rolled it round his tongue appreciatively.

Mrs Oakleigh had one further worry. "I only hope the baby looks like Robert."

"I'm sure it will," Dr Oakleigh had said confidently.

Outside the church the photographer had finished taking pictures. "Where are they going?" asked Marjorie Mayfield as the bride and groom turned and walked across the grass towards the graves at the side of the churchyard.

"To visit her sister's grave, I suppose," said her husband.

"*On her wedding day?*"

"Yes, look," he said as the bridal couple stopped at the headstone that bore the name: GEORGETTE HABEN-HOWE. The bride was smiling and holding her groom's hand but she seemed to be speaking to the grave and not to him.

Among the older villagers who were watching there were some who had no doubts in their minds what was going on. They were the crones who hovered on the edge of any such gathering in Tanniford. They were to be seen at funerals and weddings alike, devouring the scene and raking the faces of those present to provide material for their gossip. The Habenhowe twins had been their favourite victims. The mother's funeral. The first twin's funeral. And now this one's wedding. The ghouls wouldn't have missed this for the world. They drank in every detail of the scene on the far side of the churchyard.

"Did you ever see the like of it?" one old woman muttered, hugging herself with pleasure. "Right after she's married him too."

"She's offering his soul to her twin sister, that's what she's doing," another one said with satisfaction.

What, in fact, was happening as Robert and Georgette stood holding hands by the grave was nothing very dreadful. Unusual, yes, but then the Habenhowe twins had always been unusual—it was one of the things about them that fascinated people.

"Robert's here, Georgie," Georgette was saying. "It's all worked out beautifully, hasn't it? I love him . . . he loves me . . . and we both love you." She pulled a flower from her bouquet and, stooping down, laid it beneath the headstone. "You'll never die, Georgie, not while I'm alive. We're one and the same." She straightened and stood looking down for a moment. She turned.

"Kiss us, Robert," she said. "Kiss Georgie and me."